THE MOOSE

A Story of Survival

Eric Viall

Viall Books

To Elsie B. and Margaret E.
May you live
lives of
adventure.

CONTENTS

PROLOGUE

Elizabeth was sitting in her parent's house. It was the first week of April. She was cleaning her shotgun in preparation for the upcoming spring turkey season. The window was open and she heard a small airplane fly over. Suddenly she was back in the woods.

The first night was the hardest. Elizabeth had wet clothes, wet shoes, and only a survival blanket to keep her warm. She slept only in fits and starts. The ground was hard and cold. All she had was time to think about the events that had put her in this situation.

DAY 1

The day started with excitement in Fairbanks, AK. Elizabeth and her dad would be getting on a Super Cub to fly out for a moose hunt on the Yukon River in Alaska. The hunt was her graduation present. She had been hunting with her dad for the past ten years and they had always dreamed of a big adventure before she went off to college. The brochure for the hunt had been in a card he left in her room after her graduation party. He had set it on her dresser and not said anything. She circled the dates on her calendar then went and gave her dad a big hug.

They worked on her shooting and outdoor skills all summer. Elizabeth could make a fire without a lighter, navigate a river using a raft, and put three bullets in a one-inch ring at one hundred yards. They had loaded up her dad's pickup the day before their flight. Her mom had dropped them off at the airport in Bismarck. The flight from North Dakota to Fairbanks had been uneventful and an Uber took them to the hotel. They had gone out for pizza and wings since they would be eating freeze-dried meals for the foreseeable future. Their guide picked them up at the hotel the next morning.

Their excitement was palpable at the airport. Father and daughter had sorted their gear into separate piles.

Dad said he would go out on the first plane so she would not be in the bush alone. Elizabeth watched his plane take off and listened to the engine droning as it disappeared over the horizon. Her excitement cooled and she thought about the flight. She had never been on a small plane like this and it was making her nervous. First, she tried to ease her anxiety with her phone. She took a selfie in front of her pile of equipment and posted to Snapchat and Instagram. She included the hashtags: #alaska, #moosehunt, #adventure, #daddydaughter, and #womenwhohunt.

She still felt anxious, so she busied herself with a checklist. She checked that her rifle case was properly secured. She powered up her inReach device, which made a jolly sound as it powered on. She noticed that the battery was low and plugged in the device to charge. She secured two lighters in the side pocket of her pack repeating, "two is one and one is none," as she worked. Finally, she snugged down the straps to bundle everything in place. A bit calmer, she sat down and started to read the book that she had brought while she waited for her plane to arrive.

The plane was back before she knew it. It was a small single engine plane with large rubber wheels for backcountry landing. She helped load her backpack, the food, her gun case, and tent. They stored the fuel for the stove in an external compartment for safety. Elizabeth would sit behind the pilot and her gear would ride behind her. She finished loading her supplies and climbed into her seat; it was so cramped! She didn't know how her dad had managed to fit. Her shoulders only had a few inches on either side and her knees almost touched the pilot's seat. The pilot handed her a headset with a microphone so they could talk over the engine noise.

The engines roared to life and she heard the pilot talk to the control tower in her headphones. "Be advised of potential bad weather heading in from the west," the voice on the radio stated.

"Copy. I checked the forecast and think we can make it before we get blown out," the pilot responded.

"Copy, you are clear for takeoff." After they taxied out to the airstrip, the pilot squared the plane with the runway. He pulled the throttle out all the way and they sped down the runway. Elizabeth felt the wheels of the plane leave the ground. She watched the surroundings fall away from them as the plane gained altitude. The city seemed to slip by and they were quickly flying over the green carpet of the forest.

The pilot set his heading northwest toward Fort Yukon. Their total flight time was approximately one hour. About fifteen minutes into the flight, Elizabeth started to notice menacing clouds in the west. The pilot studied the clouds and radioed the tower that he was correcting his course further east to avoid the bad weather. The radio crackled and she heard the voice from the tower say, "Copy course alteration." He gave the new heading to the control tower and then set the plane to the new heading.

They flew for another twenty-five minutes, but the weather was catching up with them, even after the heading adjustment. The plane was starting to jump around due to wind gusts that were coming off the front. "Shit!" the pilot yelled. "I'm not sure we're gunna to make it. I'm going to try turning back." Elizabeth heard him try to make radio contact, but she only heard static when the tower tried to reply. The pilot banked hard right to bring the plane back around to the southeast. At that moment, a flash of light stunned them both. The flash was accompanied by a thunderous boom that left Elizabeth's ears ringing.

The pilot was fumbling in the seat ahead of her. She peeked over his shoulder. He was tapping one of the instruments on the panel in front of him. "We lost the instruments in the lightning strike," he said over the headphones. "Tower, can you read us? This is flight 452 heading to Fort Yukon. We've been hit by lightning and have lost our instruments." The silence that followed was deafening. He tried again and again. He pulled out a manual compass from his pocket and read the heading over the radio. He set the plane on a generally southeast heading and started to talk to Elizabeth.

"I think we're in trouble here. The plane was hit by lightning and I'm not sure of our exact location. The radar tower should be able to pick us up, but I don't know if the storm interfered with their equipment. We will continue on this heading, but we don't have unlimited fuel."

Elizabeth's anxiety spiked. The pilot was visibly shaken and he was saying things she didn't want to hear. She looked ahead and closed her eyes. She started to calm herself with box breathing, which a teacher had taught to her to fight her test anxiety: inhale four seconds, hold four seconds, exhale four seconds, and hold four seconds. After a few rounds, Elizabeth opened her eyes and looked around again. They were in the storm. She could no longer see the ground and the pilot was flying by the compass on his lap. He was starting to sweat as he was trying to keep their heading in the gusty winds.

"I'm going to have to go low and try to find a place to set down." He started his descent, but they must have been flying lower than he thought. Suddenly, the plane jerked hard to the left and the pilot swore. "We just hit a tree! Hope we didn't lose a wheel." They continued on just above the trees,where the visibility was better. A clearing appeared in the trees ahead with a lake just below. "I'm gunna try set her down on the lake." He banked around the lake and lined up the nose with the center. The lake was not long. "Brace for impact," she heard through her headphones.

The next moments were a blur. Elizabeth saw the lake approaching in front of the propeller of the plane. The clearing was approaching quickly through the rain pounding the windshield. The lake grew larger as the plane lost altitude. Soon, they were just over the water. Elizabeth doubled-over to put her head between her knees. The plane struck the water with a jolt and immediately pulled hard left due to the lost wheel. The plane tilted too far and the left wing hit the water. The added drag from the wing caused the plane to flip onto its top. They were skidding across the lake upside down. The last thing Elizabeth remembered was the shore and trees coming at them quickly. She closed her eyes and heard a loud crash and was knocked unconscious.

When she came to, Elizabeth was upside down in the plane with her ponytail in the water. The front of the plane was submerged and the pilot was sitting in front of her with his arms and hair floating in an eerie way. She took a quick inventory and tried to unbuckle from the seat. Her weight pulled against the clip, which prevented it from releasing. Elizabeth tried grabbing the seat between her legs and pulling herself up, but to no avail. Finally, she put her hands on the ceiling and realized she could push herself into the seat to ease the tension on the seatbelt. Pushing with one hand, she used the other to unbuckle.

Elizabeth screamed at the sudden shock of the cold water and struggled to get the door handle open. Finally, she pushed up on the door handle and the door flopped open. She jumped out onto the wing. She glanced back into the cabin and happened to notice a first aid kit. She reached back and grabbed it. The rain was still falling as she assessed her surroundings. She was going to have to get back in the water to get to shore. She jumped into the cold water and swam with all of her might toward shore. Her clothes made her feel heavy, but she finally reached a spot where she could touch the bottom of the lake. She waded the rest of the way to shore.

Elizabeth turned back and looked at the plane again. It was resting on its roof with the left wing bent at a strange angle. The left wheel was nowhere to be seen. The nose and front half of the cock-pit was submerged, but the tail was sticking up out of the water. The rain was starting to let up and the sky was clearing. She figured that the clear side was west, since that was the direction from which the storm had approached. She needed to make a plan, but the panic kept boiling in the pit of her stomach. She sat down on the beach and cried. The tension of the storm poured out of her body with each sob.

Eventually, she stopped crying and looked around. She felt weak, but stood up and tried to walk a bit. She only made it to some trees. She looked down and realized she was carrying the first aid kit. She popped it open and looked inside. It was pretty basic: bandaids, Neosporin, and tweezers. However, she did find an emergency blanket. She ripped the plastic open, shook out the blanked, and wrapped it around her body. She looked back toward the plane and burst into tears again. The full emotion was finally settling; she had almost died. She was lost in the Alaskan wilderness. Her dad was naive to her situation. It was all too much and it just flowed out of her. She curled up in the blanket and cried until she drifted off to sleep.

Elizabeth woke up as the sun was hitting the horizon. It had stopped raining, but her clothes were drenched. She needed to find better shelter and try to dry out. She got up and started to walk counterclockwise around the lake. She made it almost a third of the way around when she found a small overhang. It was an area where a giant granite rock jut out of the ground. The rock was on the edge of the woods. It was enormous; bigger than anything she had seen in North Dakota. It rose high in the air and at the base there was a space that was big enough for her to lay down and curl up. She fit snugly into the spot.

She took off her outer layers. Luckily, she had worn her wool base layers in the plane. She hung her sweatshirt and pants to dry. She searched the pockets of her wet clothes but did not find a lighter. "Okay, gunna be a cold night," she said aloud. The sound of her voice surprised her. She wrapped the blanket around her again and lay down. The ground was hard. She stood again and walked over to one of the small pines to collect some branches. She tried to break the stems, but the green wood only bent in her hand. Eventually, she managed to gather six good branches. She carried the pile over to the rocks and arranged the boughs into a bed. She lay down and closed her eyes again. She suppressed the panic to the back of her mind.

Wet clothes, wet shoes, and only a survival blanket for warmth made the first night miserable. Sleep came in fits and starts interrupted by the cold, hard ground and replays of the events of the day.

DAY 2

Elizabeth awoke to a clear, calm morning. She shrugged off the blanket and looked around. The plane was still sitting on its top in the water. Luckily, her hunting gear was in the tail of the plane, which was high and dry. Her gear had camping equipment, her hunting rifle, and most importantly freeze-dried food.

She walked to the shore and tested the water with a bare toe. It was cold but swimming was not out of the question. "How will I get it all back to land?" she said aloud again. She needed to pee and was starving. She relieved herself in some bushes, but would have no food until she solved the problem of retrieving her gear. Swimming was the only choice and she scanned her surroundings to make sure no one else was around and laughed when she caught herself. Then, she stripped off the wool base layers and hung them with the rest of her clothes. She swam to the plane in her underwear.

Elizabeth climbed on to the wing she had jumped from the day before. She rocked back and forth a bit to make sure the plane was stable. Then stepped through the door and saw that the tail was not quite as dry as it seemed. The bags had shifted to the ceiling during the crash and water had worked its way up to them. She slid them along and floated them out as best she could.

She made sure to get her backpack and rifle case. She also looked for the bear proof tote that held the freeze-dried food. She had everything out of the plane and was sitting above her seat, when she turned around and saw the pilot.

He was slumped in his seat. He appeared to be sleeping like an astronaut. His arms were floating in front of him and his eyes were partially closed. She suppressed the urge to vomit as she stared at the scene in front of her. Elizabeth had never seen a dead body at a funeral, much less up close and personal. "Who was his family? How old was he?" she thought as she looked at the lifeless body in the plane. Finally, she looked away and attempted to ignore the body.

Elizabeth looked at the pile of soaked gear around her feet and knees. "The raft!" she screamed. They had planned on packing out moose meat on small inflatable rafts. She grabbed the pack and rummaged around until she found one. She dug the yellow piece of plastic out of the bottom of a bag. She looked it over and frowned. It was folded and soggy. It needed to be opened and inflated, but how?

First, she tried to find how to unfold the raft. It had more folds than an origami swan, but eventually it was spread out on the wing. Next, she found the valve and inspected it. It looked like a twist top, but when she tried it, the top just spun. She feared breaking the valve. After a second look, she could see a space beneath the cap to pry. However, she was wary of how violently to pry the flimsy device. She stuck her thumbnail in the space and tried to remove the lid, which flew off and landed in the water. Luckily, the plastic bobbed on the surface. She lunged for the piece, but it tipped and sank. She slid her hand beneath it and captured it as it sank. She let out a long sigh when she caught it. "That was close," she said aloud.

The raft was ready for inflation. She focused on forcing her breath into the raft and tried not to think about the fact that her body was the only one in the plane able to blow air into the raft. She was at the point of exhaustion by the time the raft was inflated and rested on the wing to catch her breath, but the wind on her wet skin spurred her to action.

Next, Elizabeth put the pack, food, and rifle case on the raft. "The fuel!" she shouted. It had been stored in a special container on the bottom of the plane. She got it open and tossed the canister in the raft as well. The raft was ready to take back to shore. She pushed the raft from the wing into the lake, where it bobbed next to the wing. She gently rocked the raft and it felt stable.

Elizabeth jumped in the lake and assessed how she would swim the raft to shore. First, she grabbed the rope of the raft and tried to swim one armed, which wore her out in about 10 yards. Next, she tried to tie the rope around her waist but it was too short and she couldn't kick without hitting her heels on the raft. Finally, she swam around the side and pushed from the back, which worked best. She was making good time until the wind picked up and started to blow her away from camp. She decided against fighting the weather and headed in the direction of the wind. She landed a couple of hundred yards downwind from her camp. She was exhausted from the effort added to her hunger from not eating for over a day.

She dragged the raft onto shore and collapsed. She lay on the grass and caught her breath. Next, she crawled over to the raft and found the food bag. She opened it up and found a dry bag with a bunch of granola bars. She took a bar, ripped the package open, and ate it so fast it was gone before she had tasted much. She opened a second bar, and took her time eating it. However, her hunger was not satisfied when it was gone. She grabbed a third bar, but hesitated. This was her only food and it needed to be conserved. She placed the last bar in the bag and repacked.

She lay back on the grass and enjoyed the warm sun on her skin. She looked at the sun's position to estimate time. It appeared to be late morning. In addition to the sun's warmth, Elizabeth started to feel insects on her skin. The mosquitoes were covering her body. She found some spray in the packs and applied some to her bare skin. She hiked back to camp with a bag then dressed in her base layers again as a second defense against the bugs. She lay down to rest again before getting the rest of the supplies to the rock and fell asleep. She slept hard and startled awake forgetting where she was. She sat up and oriented herself. She needed to get the materials over to the camp. She ate another granola bar while ferrying her gear to the rock.

Once back at camp, she needed to organize everything. First, she needed to dry out the clothing and camping gear. She pitched the tent in the sun and hung all the clothing and sleeping bags from the trees. Finally, she put all the food in a bear proof tote and put it in the rock overhang. She planned on sleeping in the tent for shelter from the bugs, so she needed to store the food in a different location. Finally, she got the keys from her bag and opened her rifle case. The padding was wet, but the rifle appeared fine. The ammo was still packed in the blue plastic sleeve they had put it in when they left North Dakota.

She picked up the gun and worked the bolt action, which was functional. She pulled it up to her shoulder and aimed the scope at a rock. She slowly exhaled and squeezed the trigger until she heard a sharp click. The gun seemed to work properly, so she would have a way to get food if an opportunity presented itself. She grabbed three shells and loaded them into the magazine. Now, she would be ready if a deer or moose emerged from the forest.

Elizabeth found the water purification system in one of the packs. She had not had a drink since just before the flight the day before. She assembled the device and walked to the lake's edge. She tossed the intake and started to pump. A stream of water came out of the hose and she lapped greedily at the cold water. She drank until she was full and had to sit down. She almost felt sick. She lay back and felt the sunshine while she let her stomach settle. Then, she walked back to camp.

Elizabeth started to go through the pockets of her backpack and found a few other odds and ends. A bit of rope, a compass, some waterproof matches, and a mirror. She thought about the inReach device and screamed with excitement. She had forgotten that it was in the bag and quickly opened the pocket where she had packed it at home. Her heart dropped as she saw an empty pocket. She screamed at the frustration and could picture the device sitting at the airport charging while she waited for the plane. Elizabeth collapsed on her back crying, her whole body retching with sobs.

She cried for a long time, but finally drifted off to sleep again. She woke as the sun was just touching the tops of the trees. She was still angry with herself, but needed to get her shelter together before the sun went down. She hurried around getting the tent properly staked and the rainfly in place. She secured guy lines with stakes. She collected the dry sleeping bag and grabbed a coat for her pillow. Then, she went to the cave and opened the food box, and inspected its contents. Most of the food was freeze-dried. All of the instructions stated to add boiling water, but Elizabeth had no firewood and had not found the stove. She decided to solve that problem in the morning. She grabbed another bar and some dried fruit, then secured the lid of the container again. She walked over to her tent and crawled inside.

Elizabeth took one last look around camp. It was starting to look lived in, but it needed more organization in the morning. She needed a bite to eat and a good night's sleep. She zipped the tent closed and sat on her sleeping bag to eat her spartan meal. Last, she lay down in her sleeping bag and rolled over to snuggle in. The hard ground reminded her to find the sleeping pads in the morning. Sleep enveloped her before she had time for another thought

DAY 3

Elizabeth woke the next morning sore and twisted. She sat up and took a look at the tent walls. She was oriented, but felt adrift without a morning routine. So she got dressed. Next, she stood and looked at a bunch of packed bags that needed to be organized. However, biological urges needed attending. She was hungry, thirsty, and needed to pee. She relieved herself in the bathroom bush and collected another bar from the box. She also needed a drink. She picked up the filter and walked down to the lakeshore. This time she was much more conscious about how much water she drank. She took a few draughts from the hose and stopped. She still felt thirsty so took a couple more.

"I need to get water for camp," she said aloud. Again the sound of her voice startled her. She had not realized how quiet it was in the forest. Now she was particularly aware of the quiet. She laughed at herself again. She still had to get water back to camp, but how. She did not think she had a bucket. There were water bottles somewhere. She needed to conduct an inventory of her equipment. So she sat down to start.

Several hours later Elizabeth had everything laid out. Her supplies included:

- 2 - two-person tents

- 1 sleeping bag
- 2 water bottles
- 1 water filtration system
- 2 tarps
- 1 sleeping mat
- 2 sets of women's outdoor clothing

She had everything that she would need for a comfortable stay at camp. There were two tents because her dad's tent did not fit well in the backpack. She had taken it with her separately since she was smaller. She set up the second tent to act as a supply tent to keep clutter down in the first. The rest was what she had packed for hunting. She set up her sleeping tent with this material then went back to her pack to explore the pockets of her bag.

- 1 Compass
- 2 trekking poles
- 50' parachute cord
- 1 box of waterproof matches
- 2 Bic lighters
- 1 package of baby wipes
- 1 roll of toilet paper
- 1 bottle of soap
- 1 Mosquito Net
- 1 signal mirror
- 1 first aid kit with simple drugs
- Bug Spray
- Handsaw
- 1 moose calling tube
- Journal and pen

There was plenty here to help make her stay more

comfortable. Elizabeth placed the material around the supply tent, except for the bug spray. She stored the spray in her sleeping tent. Next, she inspected the rifle case again. She found the rifle and a case of 20 cartridges. This was plenty to last until she was rescued. Finally, she opened the bear vault and found the following food items:

- 3.5 boxes of granola bars
- 2 baggies of dried fruit
- 10 freeze-dried meals
- 1 camp stove
- 2 cans of fuel
- 1 mess kit

Elizabeth surveyed all of the supplies. She knew that survival was possible, but food would become an issue in a little over a week. Additionally, her hunting clothes were warm, but they were no match for an Alaskan winter. The days were getting shorter and nights colder, but that would be a problem for later. For now, she needed to organize and store the gear she had. But first, hot food. She had lived exclusively on granola bars and dried fruit. She needed something more substantial.

The bowls of the mess kit doubled as pots. She took them down to the lake edge and scooped up some water and carried them back to camp. Next, she needed to figure out how to run the stove. She had set it up once with her dad, but he had made most of the connections. She inspected everything. She knew the tank needed to be pressurized somehow, and then the canister connected to the burner. She fumbled around for a while and reached into her back pocket for her phone. She panicked when it was not there. She didn't know where it was. She ran over to the clothes hanging from the tree and rummaged through the pockets but did not find it. It must still be in the plane or it fell out while she swam for shore right after the accident. She sat down and screamed again. If only she had it she could look up how to assemble the stupid burner. She cried until it dawned on her that she would be unlikely to get 5G in the Alaskan backcountry.

She walked back to the stove and took a breath. She studied the openings and attachments. Finally, she recognized that the nozzle would connect to a fitting on the stove. She pushed and felt it click home. Next, she examined the tank. There was a large red knob that she tried to pull, but nothing budged. She tried to twist the knob. Once it was loose, she was able to move it up and down. She could feel the pressure building behind the pump.

Next, she studied the burner again. This time, she found a dial and turned it. It made a hissing sound, which grew louder the more she turned it. She turned off the stove and ran to get one of the lighters from the supply tent. She returned, gave the knob a couple more pumps, then flicked the Bic. She held the flame close to the burner and turned the dial again. The hissing was followed by a small whoosh. Orange flames leapt high in the air. She adjusted the dial until a nice blue flame formed in a ring around the burner. She set the metal bowl on the burner and went to find her meal.

Elizabeth sorted through the freeze-dried meals. They all sounded great after only granola for the past couple days. There were curries, spaghetti, lasagna, and stroganoff. She chose a package of lasagna and turned it over to read the instructions. She ripped open the package and waited impatiently for the water to boil. Finally, it was bubbling and steaming. She carefully picked up the bowl using a hand wrapped in her sleeve. She dumped the water into the package and sealed it. The instructions said to wait at least 5 minutes before eating. She tried to busy herself with other chores, but the thought of hot food was too distracting. Finally, she sat down and counted. She made it to 500 before she allowed herself to open the packet.

Fragrant steam rose out of the packet immediately. The savory tomato and beef smell caused her stomach to pang and her mouth to water. She scooped out the first bite with a fork and ate a bite of salty food, which caused a sensual explosion. Nothing had ever tasted so good. She took two more bites quickly, then paused. She remembered the stomach ache from drinking too much and did not want a repeat after eating. She slowed down and tried to force herself to save the food for later, but she was just too hungry. She ate the whole pouch in one sitting. She was full, but felt better. She sat back and looked out over the lake. She allowed herself to feel some hope. They would be looking for her. She had plenty of supplies and could stretch her food out for almost two weeks. She just needed to stay put and try to make the best of it. She got up and took a drink from the water filter. Now, she needed to get to work.

She would cook and clean up near the supply tent, which was set up about 100 yards away from her sleeping area because she knew that bears could be attracted by the food. She hung her food in a tree another 100 yards into the woods. Next, she went down to the water and filled all of her water bottles with filtered water. This way she would have some clean water on hand. It was coming together. She made herself a cup of hot water and ate a granola bar. The sun was beginning to set so she finished her water and splashed the inside of the cup. She put the wrappers of the bars she had eaten in a ziplock bag and set them in the woods. Finally, she crawled into her sleeping bag and curled up. She was full of hope and optimism as she drifted off to sleep.

DAY 4

Elizabeth was startled awake in the dark by a crash of thunder. Moments later she heard the light patter of rain starting. She rolled over in her bag satisfied that she had packed everything away and was in a dry place for the rain. She started to drift off when the wind came.

Suddenly, the wind was driving rain into the tent walls. She was staying dry, but thunder was booming down on her and lightning was causing a strobe effect in the tent. She was getting nervous. She had never weathered a storm outside before. The little anxious voice in the back of her mind started talking. *Do tent poles attract lightning? What if a tornado happens? Did I fasten the guylines on the tent?* The storm continued to rage. The wind howled, thunder crashed, and lightning flashed.

Elizabeth had felt so confident just a few hours earlier, but now in the dark, she felt vulnerable. The anxiety in her chest rose, and soon she was in a full blown panic. She started to sob and shiver at the same time. She didn't know what to do. The storm had probably only lasted a few minutes, but it felt like an eternity to her. The cold air, flashing light, and earth-splitting noise merged to overwhelm her senses and she curled into a ball and screamed. She screamed until the strobing lightning strikes stopped and the booms of thunder turned to distant rumbles. She was worn out and cold, yet her sobbing continued.

"I need to get up," she thought aloud.

She was starting to feel cold but had calmed down. The sleeping bag draped over her and she lay shivering as the gray morning light slowly illuminated her surroundings. It would be so easy to just close her eyes. Then, Elizabeth remembered her parents and the dorm room that was waiting for her just after Labor Day.

"No!" she screamed. She would get up and assess the damage. She would see her parents again and go to school. She got up and crawled out from the tent. She looked over at the supply tent and her heart sank. The tent was erect, but the rain fly was flipped over the leeward side of the tent. She dropped her sleeping bag, ran over and opened the door. The floor of the tent was flooded and the equipment stored in the tent was bathed in lightly lapping water.

She screamed and swore. She kicked the tent and punched the sides. Finally she sat down and cried again. She just kept messing things up. At last, hunger pulled her out of it. She sat up again. "Okay, what can I do?" she said to herself. She would need to dry everything out. Then, she would need to figure out the rain fly. Elizabeth looked to the east and the sky was fully light, but the sun was still behind the trees. The mosquitoes were starting to bite her bare skin. She needed the spray again, so she went to get it from the tent.

The bug spray was in her sleeping tent so it was dry. She gave her head a healthy dose and went back outside. Next, she needed to relieve her bladder and get some food. She made her way over to the bushes to pee, then continued to the food bin. She untied the cord holding the food in the tree but the rope did not move. She looked up at the trees and saw that the container had gotten tangled in the tree. She walked back to camp, defeated.

* * *

The flooded tent was a pretty easy fix. She simply unstaked the tent, opened the door, and slowly tipped it up so the water poured out. She laid out all of the soaked gear on the rocks above the overhang. Next, she re-staked the tent and left the door open to dry out the inside. Elizabeth examined the rain fly. She noticed some small velcro straps that she had overlooked the night before. They lined up exactly with the tent poles. She draped the fly over the tent and reattached the hooks. Then, she looped the velcro around the tent poles. She retied the guy lines and put a rock over the stakes, since they had been pulled out of the ground in the storm. She stood back, inspecting her handiwork, and her stomach growled loudly.

Elizabeth needed to untangle her food from the tree. She looked through the supplies and found the hand-saw from one of the packs. The trees where she had tied up the food were not very thick. Climbing was out of the question because the first limbs were far above her head. She thought she could cut down the tree to get the food out of the tree. She had never cut down a tree before, but how hard could it be?

With the saw in her hand, Elizabeth took off for the tree. She made it in just a few minutes. She looked up and saw that the food bin had been tangled around another tree, which needed to be cut down. She looked up at the tree and then ran her eyes along the trunk; it was maybe seven inches in diameter. She figured that she could just cut it off and let it fall. She started by sawing on the back side of the tree. She pulled a couple of short strokes to start the cut then started to go back-and-forth in the established groove. Soon, Elizabeth had a cut about an inch deep in the tree, but she quickly tired out. Poor sleep and inadequate food over the past three days emerged as exhaustion after the sudden exertion of energy. Additionally, the saw handle was hurting her hands. She needed a pair of gloves, but they were back at camp with the rest of her spare clothes. The thought of walking back made her head hurt.

She steeled her nerves and set a goal of another inch. She started sawing. Her arms burned, her hands felt hot. The saw was moving slowly toward the spot she had picked. The burning in her arms was starting to become unbearable. Elizabeth felt a blister starting to form on the palm of her right hand. The steel teeth of the blade moved a millimeter further with each pull, and each pull felt like it would be the last she could muster. Finally, the teeth grazed the mark she had chosen and she collapsed to her knees.

She was breathing heavily and the burning in her arms raged from the effort. She tried to control her breathing and let her muscles rest. Elizabeth was a little over a quarter of the way through the tree. She was not sure she could continue, but she would have to try and push through to get her food. She slowly regained control of her breathing and felt the burn of her muscles subside. She grabbed onto the handle of the saw again and started to move it back and forth. This time she attempted to control her strokes to conserve energy. She focused on every stroke and tried to breathe in rhythm with her movements.

After a few more strokes, Elizabeth found that she was more than half way through the trunk of the tree. She also noticed that the gap behind her saw was getting larger. The wood was starting to make popping noises. Finally, she noticed a lean in the tree and there was movement as the tree started to tip. Elizabeth took the saw out of the tree and backed up while it fell. There was a lot of crashing and noise, then sudden silence. She looked in awe at what she had accomplished. She folded the saw back up and stuck it into her pocket. Then, she went over to the bear canister and sat down next to it. She took out one of the meals and a bar. After eating the bar, Elizabeth stood and untangled the rope from the tree and rehung the bear canister from another tree.

Elizabeth set up her camp stove back at camp. She went to the lake and filled the pot with water, then struck the lighter over the stove. The whole stove screamed to life and, soon, she had a steaming pot of water. She let the water boil for an extra minute to make sure it was safe since she hadn't filtered it. She opened the pouch of freeze-dried food, while reading the front. "Chicken Marsala," it said in bright red letters. She dumped in the appropriate amount of steaming water and sealed the bag back up, letting it sit for a few minutes to rehydrate. She took the pot of hot water to drink as the low sun made the air slightly chilly.

She looked out over her camp again and breathed the warm steam coming off the liquid. Besides the drying equipment strewn about, it was looking better than it had that morning. She took a drink of the warm liquid and watched the sun move toward the trees forming the horizon. Finally, the food was rehydrated, and Elizabeth found herself enjoying a hot meal. She was feeling tired, but content, after the long day. She finished her meal and the last of the warm water. She packed the dry materials into the supply tent and squared them all away. Finally, she made a final trip to the bear canister to store her garbage. On her return, she crawled into the tent, slipped off her outer layers, and wrapped into her sleeping bag for the night.

DAY 5

Elizabeth woke to the song of birds the next morning. She had slept through the night and finally felt rested. She sat up and stretched. There was a grey light filtering through the nylon of the tent and she could see her breath. She rolled out of bed and put on her pants, a long sleeve t-shirt, and a puffer jacket from her pack. Then she stuck her feet into her boots and went outside. She had to pee, but the cold did not feel inviting. She decided to hold it. She went to the lake and filled her pot of water again then lit the camp stove. Setting the pot to heat would give her something warm to drink. She relieved herself on the way to the bear canister. She arrived back at camp to a steaming pot and went to work making breakfast.

After she finished her granola bar and drank the hot water, Elizabeth sat back and realized that she did not know what she was going to do. She did not have any problems to solve or messes to clean up. The idea dawned on her that she had a long wait until rescue and patience would be required. She needed to find something to do to occupy her mind. She went into her tent and found a small journal that she had brought along to document the hunt. She opened it and took the pen out of the spiral binding. "To Do," she wrote at the top and

listed the following:
- Firewood
- Shoot Rifle
- Fishing equipment?
- <u>Food!</u>

She underlined the last one. She knew that she only had eight meals left. However, she would need to figure out another source of food after the freeze-dried food ran out. She decided to tackle the firewood first. Food was a long-term problem, but staying warm or signaling a rescue was more immediate. Elizabeth got up and put the journal back in her pack. Then, she went and got the saw that she had set aside the night before.

She needed to find some dry wood. That was going to be difficult after the storm from the day before. She was hesitant to cut down another tree if it was unnecessary. She looked around the clearing but did not see much. There were not many branches immediately visible so she decided to take a hike around the clearing. The clearing was to the south of the lake. It was maybe 150 yards wide between the forest and the lake and ran most of the lake's length. Her camp had been set up on the east side, so she walked generally west, zig-zagging across the clearing.

She observed a variety of animal signs. First, she came across some feathers, which she identified as Canada goose feathers. There were some wing parts left behind with the feathers, so she figured that the bird had met a violent end. Next, she came across a pile of pellet-shaped dung. The poop looked like the deer scat at home but on a larger scale. Elizabeth bent down and inspected a pellet. She figured this was probably moose poop. She poked at it with a grass stem. The moose sign reminded her that she needed to shoot her rifle, which she filed as a mental note. She stood and continued on. Eventually, she found another pile of scat. This one looked more like her dog's poop from the backyard, except it was darker and full of hair. She figured it was some sort of predator. She kept walking for a bit, but then realized that she was in wolf country. She made another note to test the sights of her rifle when she got back to camp.

She continued toward the east, sticking near to the edge of the woods. Her goal was to gather fuel, but she was having trouble finding any wood. Most of the dead trees she saw were still standing and she was not aching to knock over another tree.

She poked around the edges of the trees trying to find some downed wood. She came upon a patch of low, brushy plants. The leaves were a yellow-green and had a pattern that looked similar to poison ivy. She stopped short. Elizabeth had no interest in being trapped in the woods with poison ivy and no calamine lotion. She was deeply affected by the rash and had ended up in the emergency room once because the rash had covered her entire lower legs. However, upon further inspection she noticed splotches of red. She bent down for a closer look. The red splotches were actually berries. They looked like the raspberries she got in the store but much smaller. The berries appeared as small clusters of BB with tiny, fine stems poking out from each ball. She picked one, crushed it, and smelled the juice. It smelled like a raspberry. She licked her fingers and it tasted like a raspberry. She decided to eat one and see what happened.

Elizabeth took one and popped it in her mouth. The berry was firm and an explosion of juice filled her mouth. The sweetness and tartness were so overpowering that her cheeks hurt. Her face wrinkled instinctively. She savored the berry and decided that they were in fact raspberries. She started grabbing berries and popping them into her mouth. She was moving through the bushes focused on finding ripe berries. There were clusters of berries all over and the patch was bursting with ripe ones. She ate her fill as she walked around the patch. She stood and took a drink of water from her bottle. She looked around to orient herself in the clearing. She had moved further along the edge of the forest to the west. She still had not found any firewood, and now the sun was high in the sky. She must have spent an hour eating berries. She walked further into the forest and sat down in the shade beneath a tree. She felt sleepy after the snack and put her head back against the trunk before falling asleep.

She awoke suddenly to grunting coming from thrashing bushes. The sounds were coming from behind the tree she was leaning against. She felt the adrenaline course through her body causing her extremities to tingle and her stomach to flip. She fought the instinct to run but she knew that running would be dangerous. She was not sure what was behind her, but it sounded like the size of a tank. She figured it was a bear.

The grunting and huffing were pronounced and getting closer. Elizabeth wished for the rifle, but she had not brought it. She knew from her reading that surprising a bear was dangerous. Although she craned her head as far as possible, she could not glimpse the sound's source. The noises came closer and closer. She was not sure what to do, when suddenly a black nose poked itself out from behind the tree. The sudden appearance of the nose caused her to scream audibly, which set off a chain reaction.

At first, the bear woofed and stood. This caused Elizabeth to jump to her feet. The two surprised individuals stared at each other for a minute. Elizabeth was quivering in fear and the bear was sniffing in her direction trying to determine what this new creature was. She screamed again, which startled the bear. Elizabeth took off toward the clearing and the bear ran in the opposite direction toward the forest. She ran until she came to the shore of the lake and turned around to see if she needed to jump in. The meadow was empty and ambivalent to her fear. She felt alone again, but now she felt weak as the adrenaline eased. Shaking, she sat down and started to cry. She felt lost, vulnerable, and sorry for herself. She let the stress of the encounter flood through her, and then it started to ebb. She calmed and stood to look around at camp.

As she regained control of her body and emotions, she remembered the list. She rearranged her priorities. It would not matter if she had firewood if she was not able to defend herself. She stood and walked back toward camp to the west. She needed to sight in her rifle, and she needed to do it today.

* * *

She lay prone over her pack. The rifle butt was tucked into her shoulder. The scope danced around the log that she was trying to hit. She had already shot twice and had made two trips to the log to see where she had hit. The last shot had been just a little high and right. Elizabeth had used the butt end of her camp fork to make the adjustments to the scope. She figured she was six inches high and four inches right. So, she clicked the dials on the turrets of the scope and reset her shooting position to test her adjustment.

She went through her motions. The cross-hairs danced as she steadied her movements, but the point of impact had started to move in a tight figure-eight around the spot on the log where she was aiming. She took a deep breath in and placed her finger on the trigger. She started to let the breath out slowly, held half her breath, and started to squeeze. She had often jerked the gun, but her work on trigger control last summer through dry-firing had helped improve her technique. She knew exactly when the trigger would break. The slow exhale had settled the cross-hairs further. She squeezed and "BOOM!"

The world exploded in front of her. She poked her head over the scope and saw that the log had moved. She opened the rifle's bolt action and set the gun at an angle so she was not walking in front of the muzzle. Elizabeth stood and walked to the log. She smiled as she saw a hole touching the small discolored portion she had been aiming for. She returned to her pack and inspected the ammunition box. She had seventeen rounds left. She would need to be careful with the gun, but at least she would have protection. Further, she would now keep the gun with her at all times.

The sun was far in the west by the time she got back to her camp. She settled in for the night with chores. She got a meal from the canister and boiled water for rehydration. Down to seven meals. Elizabeth cleaned up and made a final stop at the canister to store her trash. She visited the latrine before bed. She crawled into the tent and zipped out the world. She stripped down to her base layers, changed her socks, and then zipped herself into her bag. Her rifle was lying next to her, just in case.

DAY 6

Elizabeth awoke to the call of birds. Pale gray light filtered through the tent's nylon walls. She rose, dressed, and went about her morning chores. The work set a rhythm to her day. She would wake and visit the latrine on her way to her food cache. Then, she would go get water and boil it. Today, things were a bit awkward due to the presence of an eight-and-a-half pound rifle hanging off her back. It was strange. She had handled rifles for years, but it had always been within the context of hunting. Now, she was working with her rifle making sure it was always within an arm's length.

After camp was clean, she set out to look for firewood again. This time she took a small pot to fill with berries. She took off along the shore walking west. There was another block of granite that she wanted to climb to get a better vantage point. She walked along the shore and noticed tracks, scat, and other animal signs. She took note of areas that seemed particularly well-traveled. These may be more important if she was not rescued soon and the freeze-dried food started to run low.

It took Elizabeth a bit of hiking to reach the rocks. She was not eating as much as she would at home in order to preserve her stores, which meant she got tired easily. She stopped often to take a drink, especially during the climb. The sun was hot and the bugs were making life miserable. She used her bug spray and tried to be zen about the persistent buzzing.

Finally, she reached the top of the rocks. It appeared to be about mid-day. The sun was warm. However, the wind was blowing at her new elevation, which kept some of the bugs away. She looked around the lake again. From this vantage, she could see further to the east and west. She could see that the lake was actually fed by a river from the east and flowed west. The inlet and outlet were on either end of the lake. Due to the incoming river, there was driftwood that flowed into the lake. She saw gray bundles of sticks in different coves and eddies. The sticks had blown in and piled up. There were some along both the east and west shores. The current carried wood to the west and the wind back to the east. Elizabeth figured she could stack wood from the water and let it dry. She took note of landmarks where the wood was sitting. She planned out the afternoon. She would explore the wood piles and try to bring back some dry stuff to camp. She worked her way back down the rock. As she reached shore again, her stomach growled loud enough to hear.

"I need some food," Elizabeth said aloud. She had been talking out loud less and less as the days had gone by. She was starting to become used to the isolation, but she was still not completely comfortable. She looked to the tree line and spotted the area where she discovered the berries. She took off in that direction.

This time she knew to approach the bushes while

making noise. She would also not stick around any longer than needed. Elizabeth knew that she had been lucky the day before. A surprised bear, even a black bear, was a dangerous bear. She pulled out the pan that she brought and started to smack the bottom with the heel of her hand as she approached. She also yelled, "Hey Bear!" as she approached the spot. She did not notice any movements in the bushes, so she figured she was safe for the time being. She went about eating and picking the berries. Soon, she was full and started to fill the pan. Elizabeth stopped when it was close to full and took a sip of water. She felt like she could take a nap again before starting her afternoon's work, but she wanted to get back to camp first after the incident the day before. She made a straight line for camp and dropped the berries off by her kitchen area before going to lay down in a shady spot.

❄ ❄ ❄

Elizabeth woke, sat up, and stretched. She had a view of the whole lake shore. She looked out as she adjusted her clothing into place after her nap. She noticed a black shape around the raspberry area again and made sure the rifle was close by. She wanted to share the berries and did not have a bear license. She figured that she would be fine to shoot a moose or deer, but a predator seemed different. She wasn't ready to deal with meat yet anyway.

She took off along the lake shore past the sheltering rocks she had used the night of the crash. The pile of sticks was not too far past the area, but it was through some pretty thick forest. Elizabeth worked her way through the area slowly due to the thick vegetation. She thought it would be nearly impossible to get the wood back through the undergrowth. Finally, she popped out of the forest and was again on the lake shore. She located the wood and tried to pull some out of the tangle. It was pretty well jumbled together, so the large pieces would not budge. She set her rifle down and slowly climbed out onto the jam. There were free-floating sticks on the far side so she thought it might be easier to pull some free.

The pile felt more solid than she had anticipated, but she still carefully tested her foot placement before shifting her weight. Eventually, she found some loose logs and tossed them back to shore as she went. Some sticks were water-logged and she had a hard time getting them to shore. Elizabeth worked her way back to the shore and sat down. There were just a few sticks by her rifle. She looked at the small pile of loose wood. It would be enough for one short fire. She would need something much bigger if she wanted to signal a passing plane.

Elizabeth grabbed a stick and started to mindlessly dig in the ground. She was feeling defeated again. The forces that held the sticks in place were too strong. She needed a fuel source, but how could she use this one? Digging didn't do anything and she tossed the stick and lay back covering her eyes. When she looked up after a minute a few clouds were drifting calmly in the azure sky. She could hear the lapping of waves against the wood. The waves were driving the wood further into the bank. She sat up and uttered to the sky, "Well, I guess I can cut them free." She was not looking forward to the job. She barely got through the tree, what would this be like? Sounded like a job for later because the saw was back at camp.

Elizabeth gathered the sticks into a pile, then shouldered the gun. She tried to bend down to lift the bundle, but the rifle slipped off her shoulder and got in the way. She slung the rifle across her chest crosswise and tried again. The bundle was awkward and sticks in the middle kept slipping out. Finally, she got them secured and started off into the woods.

Bushwacking was even more difficult than before, with her new burden cradled in her arms. She ended up walking backward for much of the hike. She would start moving forward, and when she came to an obstacle, turn to use her back to spin through it. The going was slow and limbs seemed to jump out and snag her bundle. She kept dropping sticks, which required her to stop and repack, extending the trip back to camp.

Elizabeth entered camp just on the other side of the rocks she had first slept under. She dropped the bundle and heard a huff in response to the sound. Her exhausted body jolted to attention at the sound. She scanned her camp and saw a black ball running toward the trees and disappearing. She struggled with the sling and finally got the gun ready.

The bear was long gone, but the weight of the gun in her hands made her feel safe. She walked through camp carefully, her ears tuned to any sounds. Everything looked to be normal until she saw the berry pot, which was overturned with berries squashed in bear prints all around it. She admonished herself because she knew better than to leave food out. She looked back to the west and saw that the sun was touching the treetops. She needed to get her chores done before the bugs came out and forced her into her tent.

She remembered that supper was dried meal number four. She still had another six meals left, before the food situation would become dire. The day ended with only a small pile of firewood piled up in the extra tent. Elizabeth was exhausted and needed to figure out a new plan to get the wood back to camp.

DAY 7

Elizabeth awoke to frost covering the inside of her tent. She rubbed her eyes and noticed that her nose was cold then noticed breath was visible in the crisp air. She sat up and crawled out of her bed. Goose bumps instantly rose on her skin beneath her base layers. She put on her outerwear and headed for the other tent to find some warmer clothing. She shivered in her long-sleeve t-shirt as she rummaged through her bag looking for a hooded sweatshirt, hat, and gloves. Finally, she found what she was looking for and bundled up. Elizabeth felt like crawling back into her sleeping bag, but she decided it was best to get after her chores.

After breakfast, the sun had risen over the trees, and it was already starting to feel warmer. She had forgotten the rifle in the tent and chastised herself. The cold distracted her, and she had let her guard down. She retrieved the gun from the tent and set it beside her. She was cold, but she knew that chores would get her warmed up. Getting firewood to camp was her number one priority now so she could build a fire to help keep her warm. The problem yesterday had been the bulk of the wood, along with the cluttered path. She decided clearing a path would be necessary if the wood pile on the bank was her best bet.

The hand saw was in the equipment tent. Elizabeth ducked in and grabbed it and reslung the rifle over her shoulder before heading back behind the granite rock. She walked the route she had taken the day before; it was daunting. The path was only about fifty yards long but there seemed to be two-to-three branches per yard, which meant a lot of brush to clear.

"Nothing left to do but the work," she said aloud. She bent down, grabbed the first sapling in on the path, and started to cut. The job was done in about five strokes. Elizabeth tossed the limb into the forest. It was only a little over an inch-and-a-half thick, so she figured it would be useless as firewood. She hoped she wouldn't be here long enough for it to dry out. The thought, "They have to be searching for me! Right?" popped into her mind causing an instant panic. Pushing down her emotion, she moved to the next branch. This one hung at chest level. She cut it off and let it fall to the path in front of her. She picked it up and tossed it. The limb had come off fast, but it was only the second one of the day. By now she was feeling warm. She stripped off her coat, hung it on the muzzle of her rifle, and continued.

Elizabeth spent the morning cutting. She was down to just her base layer top after a few more branches. She looked behind her and saw what little progress she had made. Deflated and needing a break, she collected the gun and warm clothes, then headed back to camp. She dumped the clothes into a pile in the cooking area and slumped down next to it. Her depression was causing her anguish, which made her head hurt. Her soft coat looked inviting. She slumped over into the soft pile to rest. Elizabeth woke up some time later. She was not sure of the time, but the sun had moved a few degrees to the west. She got a snack and then restarted her project again.

Elizabeth got about halfway during her first day of work. Her hands were blistered and her shoulders ached from her efforts on the saw. She collapsed back and camp and noticed the lake sparkling as the sun kissed the tops of the trees. She used some of the dry wood to build a small pyramid in a circle of rocks. She put some small sticks and grass in the center before sticking her lighter into the grass to get the fire going. She boiled a pot of water and prepared another meal from her supply. Her freeze-dried meal tasted heavenly after the long day of cutting, but she only had five meals left.

Suddenly, the water exploded as a fish rocketed into the air from the lake. The ripples across the smooth surface were the only proof the event had actually happened. Elizabeth went through her list of supplies and found no fishing equipment. However, she noted the fish in her notebook. She cleaned up the camp before bed.

She had lingered by her fire, hoping that the frost would take down the bugs. They appeared with all their former enthusiasm and chased her into the tent. She changed base layers since she had been sweating all morning and had worn the same clothes for a week. The cool air felt good as it settled on her skin. She was tempted to sleep in only her underwear, but the memory of her cold morning changed her mind quickly. She settled into her bag, rolled over, and went to sleep to the sound of another fish splash.

DAY 8

The work of clearing a path continued the next morning after chores and breakfast. Her attack was different the next day. Starting on the camp side she would cut each branch until she got tired, take a break, then spend some time collecting the sticks and clearing the path. This seemed more efficient, and by noon she had almost reached the spot where she had left off the day before.

Her rifle was always near her, and she was meticulous about grabbing it whenever she moved ahead. It was becoming an extension of herself. She felt naked when it was not hanging from her shoulder. She had figured out how to move with the bulky item on her back. She contemplated slinging it across her chest. However, that would slow her draw. Instead, she learned to move with the rifle.

Elizabeth also noticed that her body was changing. Her hands had thick skin and did not hurt at the end of the day after using the saw. Her arms did not tire as fast and started to show the outlines of her muscles. She had long and sleek limbs, which made her feel like a predator. She envisioned her long limbs stalking through the woods and working the bolt of the rifle.

She also knew that the definition in her limbs was

coming because her body was losing its fat reserves. The soft tissue that used to hide the definition of her muscles was slowly burned to fuel her survival. She knew that she needed to start consuming more calories or else all of this work would be for not. Her food rations were holding out, but she was burning more calories than she was taking in. She needed to finish the path, so she could focus on food rather than fuel.

Elizabeth worked the rest of the afternoon and soon had the path finished from her camp to the dried piles of wood. Additionally, she had a fresh pile of wood from clearing that path in the process of drying out. She was able to make a single trip for firewood, so she could boil water for her supper without wasting the gas. She was exhausted by the time she got the flame going in a make-shift firepit.

She ate another freeze-dried meal that night. It was again delicious and she licked the inside of the bag trying to get every available calorie. She tossed the plastic wrapper into the fire and watched it crinkle and disappear. "Down to four," she said aloud, staring into the fire. She needed to get rid of her trash to keep the bears away; it was starting to cause problems in the cache. She washed her spoon and returned it to the bear bin she had hanging from her tree. She wanted to let her clothes air out, so she stripped down to her base layers and hung the clothing in the supply tent. She crawled into her sleeping bag and quickly drifted off to sleep.

DAY 9

She awoke the next day with a sense of wonder. The rain was hitting the tarp of her tent and sounded like the rap-tap-tap of snare drums. She could hear the thunder roll in the distance. Elizabeth lay in her sleeping bag relishing in the sounds of nature around her tent. Soon, nature's call drew her out of her sleeping bag. She knocked her head against the roof of the tent and water rolled off the rainfly. She expected some water to come into her tent, but the waterproofing was sound, which kept her gear dry. Luckily she had her rain gear handy in the other tent. She ran over to the tent and slipped it on before she was drenched.

She spent the morning running to and fro through the rain. She ran to the latrine. Then, she ran to her bear box for a granola bar. Next, she ran back to her sleeping tent to eat. She left her rain clothes in the vestibule of the tent to keep her sleeping bag dry. Elizabeth ate and listened to the rain. She was dozing to the sound of rain, as it started to slow to a drizzle.

She dreamt that she was hunting with her dad in the Alaskan wilderness. They were pursuing moose. She had spotted one miles away, but it had not responded to their calls. They had sat on their mountain for days glassing the wider area for moose. Periodically, they would make moose calls through a large tube to amplify the sound. The long moan of the female moose was offered up into a seemingly empty world. They were not seeing any animals in the dense woods of Alaska, but they had faith they were out there. The task of finding a single animal in the vast landscape before them seemed insurmountable. Her dad turned to her and said, "Don't give up. Believe that the animal is out there, and eventually it will come."

She woke up with a start. The rain had stopped. She could hear the water dripping from the fly of her tent. Sitting up, Elizabeth realized that she could still try to get a moose on her own. That would solve her food problem. She would set up a calling post and spend a couple of hours a day focusing on getting one of the beasts close to camp. She was almost giddy as she got up to put on her boots. She ran out in a hurry to get started, but the mist forced her to put her rain gear back on. She did not want to get her outer layers soaked.

Elizabeth went to work on setting up the calling post. The blind would be located on the southern edge of the clearing next to a large tree. It was centered east and west along the tree line so there would be equal shots no matter where an animal appeared. She could watch her camp from her post and also see everything that came out on the west side of the lake. She had not seen any fresh moose sign, but then again she had not been looking for it. The last eight days had been about survival.

The blind consisted of a pile of logs and branches, which would double as a shooting table. She set up an-

other log behind the wall for a chair. She pulled the
moose call from her pack and hung it from a branch on
the tree next to the blind. Finally, she placed a longer,
skinnier branch about the size of a baseball bat next
to her seat. The stick would be used to beat the brush
around her to simulate a moose scraping branches. By
lunch, Elizabeth was all set up and ready to try her first
calling session; however, she needed to eat first. She
went back to camp to find a bit of water and something
to eat. Lunch was generous with an extra granola bar
because she was sure she would have a hundred pounds
of meat soon. She visited the raspberry patch to collect
dessert on her way back to the stand for an afternoon
sit. She had two more granola bars to help tide her over
in the stand.

Elizabeth sat quietly to let the woods calm down
before making her first call. The call looked like a plastic
wiffleball bat with both ends cut off. Thinking for a moment about the proper sound, she raised the tube to her
mouth while taking a deep breath. She moaned into the
tube and was startled by the noise. She sounded more
like a sick bovine than a sexy female moose. She took
a breath to reset and tried again. Her second attempt
at least sounded like a healthy mammal. She sat and
waited. Her initial enthusiasm about calling blind was
being slowly eclipsed by boredom. She wanted to move.
She could feel her weight in her butt. The log seemed to
be the source of all the discomfort in the world. It was a
trial of will to sit for even a little bit. She decided to try
one more call and stood to thrash some brush.

After she sat back down, Elizabeth thought she

heard something in the woods behind her. It was a rustling noise similar to someone eating from a bag of chips. It would sound, then it would stop for a bit, and it would sound once more. This went on for ages. She sat focused on the sound that moved closer and closer to the stand. An eternity passed as the sun started to sink beneath the western trees. The sound had shifted, so that it was coming from her left. She readied the rifle as it moved toward the clearing. The animal sounded like a tank moving through the woods. She was expecting one of two animals: a moose or a bear. Either would give her food, but she was much less nervous about a moose. She rested the rifle so it was pointing to the west. She was on her knees and focused on listening. Finally, she saw some of the branches on the edge of the forest begin to shake. The animal was about to enter the clearing. She was shaking from the adrenaline flowing through her veins.

Another eternity passed while waiting for her quarry to enter the clearing. Finally, she heard it moving again. She positioned her eye in the scope and found the moving branches. Elizabeth slipped the safety off and let her finger find the curve of the trigger; she was ready. She steadied her body with long calming breaths. She caught a flash of brown on the ground and took in a big breath before the shot.

The beast was in full view, but instead of a moose filling her scope, she was disappointed to find a squirrel centered in her crosshairs. She blinked twice to adjust her sight and looked back through the scope to confirm. Sure enough, there was a bushy-tailed squirrel scurrying around in the clearing. It was busy finding seeds and putting them in its cheek pouches to bury later.

Elizabeth sighed and unloaded the rifle. She hung the call and went back to camp for supper. She had been so excited about the idea of getting a moose that the disappointment brought tears to her eyes. The small mammal and the dream about her dad had gotten her hopes up. The tears streamed down her face as she lit her fire, collected water, and boiled it. She watched the flames dance around the edge of the pot as she reflected on the day. She didn't feel like eating but forced down half a bag of freeze-dried food. She placed the rest in her bear vault and thought she would finish it for breakfast. She went to the equipment tent to store her rain gear. Finally, she went to her sleeping tent and crawled into bed. She cried herself to sleep. She was sure that her dad had tried to speak to her, but maybe she didn't get the message. She would just have to try to call a moose again in the morning.

DAY 10

Elizabeth woke the next morning with a growling stomach after not eating a full supper. She got up and quickly slipped on her outer layers. She washed her face in the lake then headed back to the bear vault to get her unfinished meal. She grabbed a granola bar as well. She thought about the dream she had of her dad while she ate the cold freeze-dried meal. It felt so real. She was sure he was trying to send her a message. She couldn't understand why she was having such a hard time getting her brain to accept that she might not get a moose on the first day. She didn't expect that from the planned hunt.

She sat with a finished bag of food in front of her. She sighed and thought about the chores she needed to get done before she could go back to the calling stand. She needed to get firewood, collect water for cooking, bathe, and wash some clothes. She had smelled herself in the sleeping bag. Elizabeth had been working in the wilderness for a week and her body was starting to sour. She had some biodegradable soap she could use for a quick bath in the lake. She collected the firewood and got a bucket of water for camp before she went to find the soap. She grabbed the soap, her other base layers, and a new set of underwear.

She stripped by the edge of the lake and looked around before she took off her underwear. Elizabeth laughed at herself again when she realized there wasn't anyone around for hundreds of miles to care about her lack of clothing. She left her clothes on the shore and would wash them later. She tentatively dipped a toe into the water. She initially jumped back from the shock of the cold water. She took another look at the water and realized this was her only option. She took a deep breath and waded up to her knees in the lake. Her skin pimpled in response to the cold, and she hurried to lather the soap, so she could get out of the cold water. She quickly washed the key areas, rinsed, and ran out of the lake. Shivering, she found the towel that she had stashed with her clothes and dried her body and shimmied back into her clothes. She noticed that her leg hair was much longer than she would have tolerated in civilization. She shrugged off the observation and proceeded to dress. Soon, she was sitting by a crackling fire to take the edge off the chill from the lake water. She looked at the dirty clothes that were piled around her. "How can you wash clothes without a machine?" she wondered aloud. Her mom had shown her how to use the washing machine, but here in the wilderness, she was out of her element.

She sat for a while and thought about how to solve the problem. "Well, I guess they had to wash clothes before washing machines. Maybe I will just have to wash in the lake."

Elizabeth gathered her clothes and headed down to the lake. She set the pile down and looked at the lake. She looked back at the pile of clothes. Then back at the lake again. She glanced back and forth multiple times trying to decide on her next step. Finally, she stooped, picked up the pile, and tossed the whole load of clothes into the water. She immediately regretted her decision.

Articles of clothing drifted in all directions and she was unsure of how to get soap onto the clothes. She had never seen how they washed laundry prior to machines. Now she had a mass of wet fabric to fish out of the lake, all while trying to stay dry. Elizabeth marched back to camp to grab a big stick from the firewood pile that she had refreshed earlier. She used it to bundle the clothing along the shore. She had grabbed her rain gear from the supply tent so she could stay dry. Finally, she had a pile of saturated fleece, base layers, and underwear on shore. The clothing was not only filthy from a week's worth of work, but now it was also covered with sand. She sat back and looked at the mess. Tears welled up in her eyes again, but this time her tears were accompanied by anger rather than sadness.

Elizabeth stood and yelled at the lake through her tears, then she picked up the stick and tossed it into the lake. She stormed back to her camp and grabbed the rifle. She needed to get to work finding food. She took the "long" way to the blind, which was a lap along the lake and then around the far side of the clearing. By the time she made it back to the blind she had cooled down. She loaded the gun, leaned it against the tree, and sat down on the log seat. The calling tube was hanging from the limb, which she unhooked and set in her lab. Elizabeth waited for the woods to settle before making her first sound.

She started out with a one long moan. The call sounded confident and clear. She produced three more decent calls, then sat back and waited. She felt her body relax into the process, which made her more patient than the previous day. Her mind wandered to the last couple of weeks and the troubles that she had overcome. Her confidence had grown as she overcame obstacles. She knew she could figure out how to do the laundry in the lake.

She forced herself to wait a half hour between calls, which was difficult to gauge without a watch. After five calling sessions, Elizabeth had an idea. She remembered an old movie that her dad made her watch where women washed clothes in a stream by beating them against rocks. She quickly scanned the shore from her blind and found a rocky outcropping that led down into the water.

She hung the calling tube, grabbed the rifle, and hurried back to camp. Once there, she rushed around putting on her rain gear, grabbing another stick, and then the soap from the supply tent. She jogged over to the pile of wet, dirty clothes, bundled it into her arms, and rushed over to the rocky point. Clothes tumbled into the shallow water along the shore. She crouched and started sorting them into piles. A dab of soap was added to each, then she spent time lathering up the clothes with her hands to build up a rich suds. Next, she beat the clothes against the rocks to get the soap into the fabric. She released her frustrations into thrashing the clothes on the rocks. Finally, a dip in the lake rinsed the soap from the fabric. Elizabeth wrung the clothes of water and set them on a clean rock to dry in the sun. Then, she returned to camp to do the evening chores while her fresh laundry dried.

Supper was much more enjoyable with her laundry success. However, she was on her seventh meal, with only three left. Hunting was going to become much more important in the next few days. Nonetheless, a sense of satisfaction swept over her as she sat in the light of the setting sun. She went back and gathered her clothes in the twilight, swatting mosquitos. Some items were still wet and needed to be hung in the equipment tent. Then she cleaned up camp. The mosquitos were becoming intolerable by the time she made it back to her tent. Her sleeping bag felt divine as she crawled in wearing a fresh set of base layers. Sleep came over her as soon as her head hit the pillow, and she slept like a corpse all night.

DAY 11

Elizabeth woke the next morning to the grey light filtering through her tent. She lay in her sleeping bag, listening to the forest wake up. She heard a beaver tail slap the water and birds call as they flew over camp. Finally she kicked out of the sleeping bag and got dressed for the day. She opened the zipper of the tent and gasped.

The supply tent was fine, but the kitchen was a mess. It looked like a small explosion had happened; her equipment was scattered in every direction. She grabbed the rifle and chambered a round out of habit. She checked the safety on the firearm and stepped out of the tent to scan the woods. She craned her neck left, right, up, and down to see if she could make out the bruin through the trees. Elizabeth strained her ears for any sign of huffing or grunting, but the woods were alive with small animal sounds. There was no sign of her visitor. She kicked the pots and pans around to create some noise during her investigation. She inspected for holes in her water pan by holding it to the light. She needed to call for moose and repairs were not part of her plan for the day. Nothing appeared too damaged. Aluminum pots had teeth marks and some surface scratches, but nothing that was ruined.

Elizabeth spent the first part of the morning reorganizing camp then went for breakfast. She stepped next to a bear track on her way to the food cache. It was enormous. The track was as long as her own foot and twice as wide. Additionally, she could see the imprints of the long claws in the mud. She reacted by slinging her rifle off her shoulder and assuring there was a live round in the chamber. She stalked her way to the food tree, keeping her head on a swivel. She was on total alert and even found herself sniffing the breeze as it moved past her nose. The heightened awareness surprised her, but she figured it was another sign she was becoming more comfortable in the woods. Pine trees and soil were the only scents she could pick out.

She finally came to the food tree and found what she expected. There was a mess of bear prints under the vault along with scratches on all the trees surrounding it. Her senses were heightened as she scanned the dense forest around her for any sign of movement. Her pulse thumped in her ears with each beat of her heart. The woods were much closer here and any confrontation would be a surprise at only a few yards. No movement caught her eye as she stood still as a statue. Finally, Elizabeth felt there was no immediate danger, and she slung the rifle back over her shoulder. She quickly gathered what she needed for breakfast from the food vault and put the food back up in the tree. After a quick retreat back to camp, she could think about what she would do for the rest of the day. She was looking down, opening a granola bar, when she stepped into sight of camp and screamed.

The bear had returned and was enthusiastically dismantling her recently organized kitchen. Her scream had alerted the bear to her presence. It was standing on its back feet with a curious look on its face. It was sniffing the air trying to catch any scent that the breeze might bring to it. Elizabeth pulled her rifle up to her shoulder in hurried but awkward movements. She had trouble finding the rapidly retreating bear in her rifle's scope. By the time she did, the bruin was retreating into the woods. The bear ducked into the thick brush along the edge of the clearing and was gone. Her arms dropped, letting the rifle fall to waist level. Her body shook from the adrenaline flowing through her body and blood pounded in her ears from her bounding heart. She took a moment to control her breathing before continuing back into camp.

Elizabeth sat facing the woods where the bear had disappeared. The rifle was resting against her legs as she finished opening the granola bar she had retrieved from the ground. It had been abandoned in the excitement while she fumbled with her rifle. There were two or three pine needles sticking to it, but it hadn't been coated in dirt. Throwing out calories was not an option, so it was consumed quickly. She had not realized it was almost gone when she took the last bite. Her focus was on the woods. They were now full of bears and other beasts in her vivid imagination. She took a breath and then continued on with her morning chores.

The afternoon moose calling session was uneventful, which was welcome after the excitement of the morning. Elizabeth estimated that she had called for a little over two hours and had spent the time between calls thinking about how to gather food from the woods. Then she remembered the fish jumping in the lake as the sun set a couple of days before . Catching fish would feed her, but how would she catch them without fishing equipment?

Elizabeth grew impatient with her calling, so she hung up the call. She was heading to her food cache thinking about fish when a grunt startled her from the woods to her right; she froze. Her body shook so intensely that unslinging the gun was a challenge. She cycled a round clumsily and sent a live round into the grass by her feet since she had kept the rifle loaded all day. She held the rifle in a ready position. The sound of blood pounding in her ears made hearing difficult, but Elizabeth thought she could hear twigs breaking as something moved away in the opposite direction. She waited, stone-still, for what felt like an eternity. Finally, she continued her walk to the food vault. She decided she would have to move the cache in the morning, but the sun was setting. She was almost back to camp when the memory of the cartridge struck. Cursing herself silently, she headed back into the woods. After a few steps, she thought differently. She turned back toward camp to make supper and finish her evening chores.

Only two freeze-dried meals remained. Wild food was going to become vital in the next few days or it would mean going hungry. She moved her pots and pans further from camp for extra bear safety. She checked camp one last time before heading for her sleeping tent.

She lay in her sleeping bag thinking about how to get fish out of the water. Finally an idea struck. Elizabeth figured that she could try to use a mosquito net to trap the fish. A rough idea for a fish trap was in her mind's eye, but she would need to gather the tools in the morning to implement the plan. Visions of her fish trap danced before her eyes as she lay in her bag trying to sleep. She visualized a wooden structure with mosquito netting stretched over it, which distracted her from sleeping well. Finally, she cleared her mind by laying with her eyes closed and absorbing the sounds of her environment. Frogs were croaking and insects were buzzing. The bird calls were intense again as the sunlight faded to an inky blue. She relaxed more with each passing moment. A calm washed over her body. She drifted off thinking about the live shell that was beneath the food vault.

She dreamt again. She was sitting in the moose stand, calling through the tube with all of her breath. She was sure that she would be successful, but she just needed to be patient. She heard the moose before she saw it. The large brown legs stomping through the brush made a slow, steady noise as it moved, which was much different from the quick noises made by the squirrel. It had a cadence that was unfamiliar but she was absolutely sure it was a moose. The bull entered the clearing on the far west side. Elizabeth had been looking at the lake and noticed the animal when she happened to look up. The moose was huge! Its antlers spread across its head and waved from side to side as the bull searched for the noisy female it had been seeking.

The rifle rose slowly to her shoulder in the dream. She could now see the bull in her scope. It was facing her, so she let the crosshairs settle on the cowlick of its chest. The body was too narrow to risk a shot so she had to be patient. Her heart pounded, which caused the scope to jump. She focused on letting the crosshairs float on the bull's body and not worrying about aiming at an exact spot. They were in a standoff. Eventually one would have to blink.

Finally, the bull turned its head right and made a step, which opened up the left side of the rib cage. Elizabeth had been waiting for this moment. She took in a deep breath, let the crosshairs settle on the ribs right behind the shoulder, and released half her breath before holding the exhale. She started squeezing the trigger on the hold and waited for the blast of the rifle. She startled awake in the dark the moment the trigger broke in her dream.

DAY 12

Elizabeth did not sleep well after waking up from her dream. All she could think about was the moose settled in the crosshairs of her scope. She tossed and turned all night thinking about what the shot in her dream could mean. Was it prophetic? Did she have a duty to try sitting for longer than usual in her moose blind? Her brain raced with activity until the gray light filtered through the canvas of her tent. She dressed quickly then headed out to make breakfast. She ate a bit of breakfast while standing, so she could take stock of the mosquito netting that she had in the supply tent.

The netting was a fine mesh and had a camo pattern. There was enough to cover a cot so there was plenty of material to work with. She also grabbed a tent repair kit that her dad packed for emergency leaks. She took her materials back to the camp kitchen and laid them out. The mesh was large enough to cover her dad's six foot frame and was shaped sort of like a balloon. The minnow traps she had seen were made to look like a cage with two funnels on each end pointing inward in the tube. The fish followed the walls of the trap to try to get out and found themselves swimming into the corner of the funnel and trap wall. She wondered if she could make something on a larger scale for trout.

She folded the fabric over itself to see if it would hold its shape. It was not sturdy enough without some sort of internal structure. There was no extra metal in the camping supplies that would work to prop the trap open. Looking around, she was trying to find something on the landscape to help her. Her eyes scanned across the lake and stopped on a patch of trees waving in the breeze on the north shore. The limbs swayed easily in the wind indicating their malleability. Elizabeth needed a closer look at the wood and decided to make a trip. However, she was apprehensive because of the bear encounter the day before.

Standing resolutely, she checked to make sure there was a live round chambered in the gun, which reminded her of the cartridge by the food vault. It had slipped her mind when she was making trips for breakfast. She also remembered that the food vault should be moved further from camp. After completing these tasks, she headed toward the opposite side of the lake along her firewood path.

Once the cleared path was behind her, the dipping, diving, dodging, and weaving through the bush made the trip much longer than she expected. She was constantly changing the position of her rifle to make it through the tight gaps in the trees. Additionally, all of the area looked the same and it was hard to keep the lake in sight at all times. She knew that the lake needed to be on her left and she needed to follow the shore, which was easier said than done. Her meandering through the woods took the rest of the morning. Finally, she crossed the river over some rocks before she found the grove of trees she was looking for on the far north side.

The trees had a small diameter and were quite flexible. Elizabeth tested some of the trees by trying to make a loop out of the branches, which she did easily. She cut five good branches that were each about six feet long. The leaves and small branches were going to be a problem, so she sat down to strip them off, making it easier to transport back to camp. She took a moment to study the leaves. They were longer than they were wide, had toothy, rough edges, and came to a point. They had a similar appearance to a weeping willow that grew in her grandparents' yard in North Dakota, she figured that they must be some kind of willow. She remembered that some of the tribes in ND made bull boats out of willow limbs and buffalo hide. Additionally, she remembered that aspirin came from willow bark. She stripped some of the bark and put it in her coat pocket. Elizabeth thought it might come in handy if she needed some pain relief.

After she finished stripping the branches, she bundled them together with bark to make it a little easier to get through the woods. She quickly realized the trip back was going to be tough sledding. Her frustration rose as she moved the branches through the woods. The long branches seemed to get tangled in every tree in the forest. The sun passed overhead and she had used up much of the afternoon before she made it back to camp.

Her lost time made her anxious so she made a quick lunch and rested before starting her construction. A long drink of water, two granola bars, and some berries relaxed her. She was laying on her back looking at the clouds when she heard a twig snap in the woods. She sat up and found the rifle in one fluid motion. She spun toward the sound and froze. She was expecting to see a bear but was surprised to see a moose standing on the edge of the clearing. Her shock prevented her from raising the rifle and she stood in awe of the enormous creature. It stood at least six feet at the shoulder and its antlers were at least that wide. They had huge scoops on each side. Jutting out from the massive paddles were dozens of points.

Elizabeth and the moose were stuck in a stand-off. She finally came to her senses and jerked the rifle up to her shoulder. The sudden movement startled the moose and it turned its huge body and retreated into the woods at a surprising speed. It had disappeared into the thick forest before Elizabeth found the safety lever on her rifle. Her heart bounded as she stood with the butt pressed into her shoulder. She did not catch another glimpse of the animal. She let the rifle drop and tears welled in her eyes as she realized she'd missed her opportunity at weeks worth of meat. She was furious with herself for moving and started a pity party.

"Why do I keep making mistakes?!" she screamed. She cried until her eyes were dry. All there was left was to do the next thing.

After her late lunch, she ordered camp after her late lunch and walked over to the fish trap supplies. Elizabeth rolled out the mesh and examined it again. She was trying to see an obvious way to build the trap. After a moment, she went to gather the willow poles. She cut the ties around the branches with her knife. She took a branch and bent it into a hoop. She stood on the ends of the hoop while she cut more strips of willow bark to tie the ends together. When she moved her foot to test the knot, the hoop retained its shape. Next, she made a second loop to keep the body of the trap open. She stuck the first loop into the top of the netting where it would hang from the tent. The hoop fit snuggly in the netting. Elizabeth placed some split sticks into this loop to act as supports. She split the other ends of the vertical sticks and secured the second loop on top. Finally, she pulled the netting up over the top loop. It fit well, but there was a bundle of extra material. She pulled it all together and thought about how to make the trap. She needed a break, so she let the material sit while she walked back to camp.

Elizabeth got some water and a handful of berries from the berry pot. She sat and looked at the water while letting her mind wander. She thought about the afternoons with her dad in the shop working and thinking on their projects. He liked to build furniture for her mom. He talked about how much money they saved, but she secretly thought that they probably cost twice as much by the time he was done making three or four cutting mistakes. Her mind returned to the present and she was ready to try the last step.

She had an idea and took three more sticks that were about one-third the length of the others and split the ends. She put those on the backside of the top loop so they were pointing into the trap. Finally, Elizabeth made a third loop out of one of the willows. Except this one was just large enough for her fist to pass through.

She fastened the small loop to the shorter sticks to make the entrance to the trap. Finally, she made a cone by pulling the open end of the fabric through the small loop and pulled it in place. Stepping back, she admired her creation. It certainly resembled a minnow trap from the store. She was confident it would work once she sewed everything in place.

The sewing took until supper. She ate quickly and returned to finish before bed. She stuck the fish trap in the equipment tent after she finished. The sun was already behind the trees. She was tired and ready for a restful night's sleep.

Before she drifted off to sleep, she thought of the moose and all the food it represented. She was down to her last freeze-dried meal. She stared up at the tent's ceiling thinking about what she would do once she had a moose laying on the ground. Would she have the skills to skin, butcher, and store the meat from something that large? The white-tailed deer at home were maybe a tenth the size and moving one of those could be difficult. Doubts rose in her mind but she was still determined to get a moose for the protein. As a final thought, she decided she would set her fish trap off the rocky point. She would bait it with berries and tie it off with a length of paracord. She fell asleep listening to the sounds of the evening. No dreams disturbed her sleep.

DAY 13

Elizabeth jumped out of bed to try her new fish trap. She slept well the night before, but now it was time to try the contraption that was sitting in her supply tent. She hurried through her morning chores and finished breakfast before the sun was over the tops of the trees. She jogged over to the tent to retrieve the trap along with a coil of paracord. The cord was tied to the back hoop of the trap and she hiked it to the rocks to make her set.

She baited the trap with some berries. She wasn't sure of the best bait, but she had berries. She tossed the baited trap into the water and tied the line to a large rock. She immediately felt impatience well up in her body. Elizabeth stared at the spot on the lake where the line entered the water. She felt the urge to pull the trap out to see how many fish she had caught already. She resisted and knew that patience was the only way to catch a fish. Images of fresh fish roasting over a bed of coals made her mouth water.

Calling moose in the blind was the perfect way to get her mind off the fish in the trap. The moose from yesterday couldn't have gone far so she jumped up, slung the rifle over her shoulder, and headed back to camp. She made sure there was enough firewood to roast the fish and chose a stick that she would use to spit the trout. Her plan was to call twelve times throughout the day. She would sharpen the stick while she waited between calls.

The day had gone slowly with no signs of ungulates. Some rustling had caught her attention in the woods behind her, but she never witnessed anything moving. As she sharpened her stick, Elizabeth thought about the fish that would come out of her trap. She realized that she had not put a door or any type of hatch in the trap but figured that she could remove any catch by sticking her arm through the entry and pulling out the fish. Her butt, legs, and lower back ached from sitting on the log all afternoon. Stretching, she stood and scanned the clearing one last time before exiting the blind. She carried her rifle and the sharpened stick back to camp to check the trap.

Her rifle was leaning against the large rock on the shore as she climbed out onto the rock. She pulled the cord gently to bring the trap out of the water and onto the rock. The weight of the trap was significant as it was pulled through the water but it became easier to pull as it gained momentum. Anxiously, she waited for the top of the trap to break the water's surface until finally she saw a rear hoop appear above the glimmering lake. This was it; she anticipated a sudden swirl of splashing tails as the fish entered the thin atmosphere. One more pull, nothing. Another pull, nothing. Finally, the whole trap was out of the water and Elizabeth grabbed a willow hoop to pull it out and inspect it.

She peered into the trap inspecting for any signs

of flopping aquatic life. However, she was sorely disappointed to find that she had not caught so much as a crayfish. She wondered if Alaska even had crayfish. A defeated feeling came over her as she let out a heavy sigh. She had gotten her hopes up again, but this time she didn't feel like crying. There was a bit of her that just wanted to lie down and quit. She didn't get any fish, she didn't get a moose, and she couldn't even distinguish a squirrel from a moose.

Suddenly, she heard her dad's voice saying, "Hard things are hard." She stood and walked over to the edge of the rock to grab the rifle. She needed more bait. Maybe fish didn't like berries. Elizabeth looked around and thought about what fish eat. At home they used worms and leeches to catch walleye, but would fish in the Alaskan wilderness eat the same? She decided to think about it over supper.

Elizabeth sat and ate her last remaining freeze-dried meal. Her need for another food source was critical. The sun was starting to dip over the trees to the west. The low angle illuminated the lake, which made clouds of bugs visible like dust floating in beams of light at home. As she was studying the swarms, a fish jumped out of the water through one of the clouds. She sat and observed the lake's surface and witnessed many fish jumping at the clouds of bugs. At one point, the lake surface seemed to be alive with activity. She realized that the fish were eating the bugs. She didn't know how to use bugs as bait, but the trap wouldn't catch any fish sitting out on the rock.

Elizabeth saved the last two bites of her chicken and

headed back to the trap. She emptied the bag into the netting and tossed it back into the water. She was hoping for some overnight activity to score some protein. She secured the rope on the anchor rock and headed to her tent.

She dreamt of her dad sitting at the kitchen table in Bismarck. They were discussing plans for the hunt. She said, "Dad, I'm worried that I won't be able to do it. What if it's too hard?"

"Hard things are hard, honey. However, hard things make life worth living. If it were easy everyone would do it. We are going to have an adventure that you can tell your kids about."

She woke up and cried a little. Elizabeth was having an adventure, but it was a hell of a lot harder than she could have dreamed. She calmed down and rolled over. She slept uninterrupted the rest of the night until the birds started calling and the gray light of dawn crept into her tent on the cool Alaskan morning.

DAY 14

The next morning, Elizabeth finished a breakfast of granola bars before checking the fish trap. She had kept her hopes subdued and wasn't expecting much. However, she didn't want to admit defeat just yet, so she went back to check for fish. She left her rifle at the bottom and climbed back up on the ledge to find the anchor. This time she noticed that the dew was dripping off the line. Drops of glistening gems scattered as the cord shook with each pull. This time, she wasn't paying attention to the trap as it emerged from the water. She felt it was a long shot to catch anything. She dropped the rope in surprise when a fish splashed as it left the water. Peering into the trap, she counted two fish swimming at the bottom of the net.

She lifted the trap onto the rock and examined her catch. The flopping fish were shining in the morning sun as they tried to find their way back to the water. A scream left her mouth as she danced around the net, celebrating her first wild protein. Calming down, she looked into the net again and wondered how to get the fish out of the trap. Her hand just fit through the opening. She slipped a finger into the gill plate of each fish. They sort of looked like the rainbow trout in the stocked ponds at home. However, they were a darker green with white spots all over their bodies. She dispatched both fish with a quick smack on the head against the anchoring rock. She did not have her knife, so she needed to get back to camp to clean them.

Elizabeth had not filleted a trout before, but she had gutted them. First, she turned the fish so it was belly up in her left hand and made a slit from the vent to the base of the gills. Next, she cut the small piece of flesh that connected the jaw to the gills. Finally, a quick tug in the opening pulled the entrails out of the animal in one movement. She flung the guts on the ground and repeated her process for the second fish. Elizabeth carried her catch to the lake's edge to wash the blood line away from the spinal column and rinse the body cavity. Back at camp, she skewered the fish on the sharpened stick from the previous day. The stick threaded through the mouth and to the back of the body cavity. She held it in place by poking two smaller sticks through the body cavity. The cavity was enclosing the stick, which was propped over the coals of her fire. She made another stick while the first fish cooked, pausing to turn the stick for even roasting.

Elizabeth grew impatient as the aroma of the fish wafted over the camp. The smell of fresh protein cooking was torture after eating freeze dried meals for the last two weeks. At last, the fish was cooked and she got to try a taste. Its skin was blackened and the eye was cloudy. She removed one of the smaller sticks and the skin peeled back with it. The flesh beneath the skin was flaky. The meat was hot on her fingers as she took a pinch to her mouth. The bite was juicy and the rich flavor filled her mouth.

The meat was mild and the oil from the fish coated her tongue. It was heaven to taste something so fresh and clean. The flesh was stripped from the bones leaving a head with a skeleton. The remains looked like the leftovers of a fish eaten in a cartoon. It was gone too soon and she sat impatiently while she waited for the second fish to finish cooking. She savored the second fish and soon her first wild-caught meal was finished. Elizabeth was left licking her fingers.

She needed to clean up camp. Disposing of the fish guts and skeletons was necessary to keep bears away. But where could she get rid of them? Additionally, she needed to reset the trap to keep the supply of trout coming into camp. A sudden realization came to her that she could bait the trap with fish guts, which killed two birds with one stone. She grabbed the pile of offal and walked back to the rock. Elizabeth fed the guts and both skeletons into the trap through the hole, then tossed the whole trap back into the lake to soak for the day. She added "checking the fish trap" to her daily list of chores morning and night. She would do it right before getting food from the vault. She walked down to the edge of the water to wash her hands again. She was full and hoped that the trap would continue to produce meals. The thought of bears was in the back of her mind, especially with the guts in the water. However, it was a chance she would have to take in order to keep a supply of food.

Back at camp, Elizabeth cleaned up the remains of breakfast with a sense of pride. She had designed and created a fish trap which had caught fish. Then, she cleaned, cooked, and ate the catch all on her own. She walked to the blind with a spring in her step.

She spent the afternoon in the blind and called in half-hour increments. Nothing had moved in the woods all day and boredom was causing her to fidget. Hanging up her call for the day and stretching, Elizabeth caught something moving out of the corner of her eye. It was along the edge of the trees. She ducked and scrambled for her gun at the same time. Adrenaline flooded her body, which caused her heart to pound in her ears and her hands to shake. She slowly raised her head over the edge of the blind, searching for any sign of big game.

The clearing was still. Nothing moved. Even the wind seemed to have calmed. A snapping twig and shaking branches to her left caught her attention. The creature crept along the grass behind some branches, ignorant of her presence. Elizabeth pointed the rifle toward the movement. She slipped the lever safety forward and placed her finger along the top edge of the trigger guard. The grass shook as the creature moved toward her. She was surprised to see a small feathered head poke up above the grass. The bird's head jerked with each step it took into the clearing. She brought the crosshairs down to rest on the bird's head. It was turning left and right scanning for danger. The bird seemed nervous but not spooked. Elizabeth moved her finger down to the trigger as the tension grew.

Her finger found the curve of the trigger. She took a breath, released half, and started to squeeze. The crosshairs settled on the head of the bird and she continued to squeeze. The world erupted with the gun's explosion.

The blast and recoil surprised her and she lost sight of the bird for a moment. She looked over the scope and was surprised to see the carcass of the bird flopping around on the ground. She jumped out of the blind and ran to the bird. The head was completely gone. The stump of the neck was gushing blood as the bird was in its death throes.

Elizabeth had killed scores of game birds back home, but never with a rifle. It was an impressive shot. She bent down and inspected the feathers. The bird looked similar to the sharp-tailed grouse at home but was brown with white feathers on its legs. Since the woods were disturbed, she picked up the bird and headed back to camp.

Back at camp, Elizabeth plucked the bird to preserve the skin. First, she pulled off all the body feathers, wings, and bony parts of the legs. Next, she headed to the fishing rock and slit the belly of the bird open. She stuck her hand inside and pulled out the intestines, which she set aside for fish bait. She was disappointed to find the fish guts untouched in the net and added the avian entrails before submerging the trap back in the lake.

The plucked grouse looked like a tiny Thanksgiving turkey. It was roasted in a similar manner to the trout. The sharp end of the stick was pushed through the wide opening in the back and she threaded the point through the neck. She had built a fire and let it burn down to coals. The bird was propped over the fire. She boiled some water for warmth as the sun sank behind the trees.

The bird tasted even better than the trout and Elizabeth went to bed with a full belly of fresh meat. She was proud of her wilderness accomplishments. She couldn't believe that she had been alone for two weeks. It felt like a day ago that she had spent the night wrapped in an emergency blanket, freezing and wishing the search and rescue plane would fly over and see her.

She sat up, realizing that she had not seen a plane since the crash. How were they not looking for her? Fall temperatures arrived in September this far north. She needed to be ready if a plane suddenly appeared in the sky. She decided to work on that the next morning before her afternoon moose hunt. She drifted to sleep thinking about trout and grouse roasting over an open fire.

DAY 15

Elizabeth was awake with the sun. She started a fire and got some water. Next, she checked the fish trap, finding another pair of trout. They were quickly dispatched and roasted for breakfast. The fish tasted almost as good as the day before. She finished her morning chores by resetting the fish trap off the rocky point.

Building the signal fire pyre was the first item on her to-do list. She wanted something that could be lit quickly, in case a small plane flew over her campsite. A large stack of wood with kindling in the middle would be most efficient. Elizabeth went to work gathering wood for the structure from her wood pile. Kindling was collected from the leftover willow branches and bark from the fish trap. Additionally, she went into the forest and cut six boughs from pine trees and drug them back to camp.

Elizabeth used large logs to build a square base. Then, she built and continued to stack the branches until she had a rough "log cabin" structure that was three feet by three feet. Next, she filled the walls with smaller sticks and dried grass. She built two more layers then added a "roof" by enclosing the structure in logs. She left an opening at the top so she could reach in to light the dried kindling. She draped the pine boughs over the roof to try to keep the wood dry. Finally, Elizabeth decided some rocks around the outside of the pyre would help contain the fire. It was midmorning by the time the work was done. Admiring her efforts, she went back to the food vault to get a snack.

She ate her granola bar in the moose blind. Elizabeth decided that she needed to spend more time on moose hunting after tasting the fresh meat from the prior day. The blind was the same as the day before. Building the pyre this morning reminded her that she had no idea where she was. There was no way of knowing how far off the plane was from its original course. She ate her snack and tried to think of anything other than the desolation of the wilderness around her.

After her fourth call of the morning, a moose appeared across the lake. She figured it was nearly noon. The animal had its head and antlers poking out of the willow thicket where she had cut the poles for the fish trap. The moose appeared to be the same as the bull Elizabeth had seen in her camp a couple of days before. The paddles seemed to glow in the sun as the bull waved them back and forth. Shifting her body with anxiety, Elizabeth was closer to a moose in her hunting blind than she had ever been. Her heart raced as her focus was centered on the animal across the lake. She felt torn about it coming back to camp. She loved seeing it out in the trees, but she desperately needed to eat. Was it fair to kill such a large animal? Would she be able process the meat before it spoiled? Wasting game meat was sacrilege to her family. Additionally, a huge, rotting carcass would attract bears to her clearing. However, she knew the moose was too far at the moment.

Elizabeth sent a long, moaning moose call out from her calling tube. The moose's head ducked back into the willows and was gone. It had not reacted as she thought. She sat still waiting for the animal to move into her clearing. The beats of her heart chronicled the passing seconds. Minutes had passed without any event. After waiting for what seemed like an hour, she let another call go from her tube. The clearing was calm. Even the birds seemed to have left.

Suddenly, she saw movement from the corner of her eye. The moose had emerged from the woods on the opposite side of the clearing from her camp. It was working its way along the edge of the water toward the pyre she had made for the signal fire. The rifle was leaning against the wall of the blind. She quickly grabbed it and worked the action to chamber a round. She slowly laid the barrel of the gun over the edge of the blind. She rested her right cheek against the stock of the rifle and found the sight picture, aligning the moose's ribs with her crosshairs. The "+" was resting just behind the front leg of the moose on the rib cage. Elizabeth flipped the safety lever forward and waited for the animal to stop. Her heart beat made the scope jump but the large animal was just over a hundred yards away, which made its flank practically fill her scope.

Finally, the moose stopped to sniff a spot in the grass. Her finger found the curve of the trigger and Elizabeth went through her shooting ritual: big breath in, release half, hold, and squeeze. The rifle roared and the moose crowhopped at the shot. It spun around on its hind legs and faced the direction it had come. She racked the bolt to chamber a fresh round while pivoting to realign her body with the animal. A wound was visible with blood dripping as the animal walked back towards the woods. Picking a new spot on the ribs, Elizabeth quickly readied herself for another shot on the opposite side. She breathed and squeezed the trigger again. The rifle roared a second time and the moose twitched at the shot. A third round was chambered, but the moose had stumbled to its knees. It laid on its side a moment later. Its long legs kicked as life left its body.

Elizabeth screamed, whooped, and jumped with excitement after taking down the moose. After the celebration, she put the rifle on safe and moved out of the blind while examining the large carcass lying near the shore of the lake. The animal was completely still as she approached it from its back and gave it a little kick. Nothing. She eased toward the head and looked into its eyes. A green sheen had already set in and its stare was fixed in the far distance. Elizabeth poked the eye with the muzzle of her rifle and saw no reaction. Kneeling next to the animal's back, she pet its broad flank. She felt the warmth of its body beneath its fur and knew she needed to remove its hide to prevent the meat from souring. Then she admired the antlers of the bull. The bases were larger than her wrist and she could just reach the tips of each antler. There were three brow tines on the bull's left side, which meant she could keep the head when she was rescued.

The shock and excitement wore off after a few minutes and all that was left was the work. Elizabeth walked back to camp to get knives, a tarp, and game bags. Getting the hide off quickly was the most important first step, but she wasn't sure how to handle the giant animal. She had watched YouTube videos of the gutless method of butchery with her dad, but had never actually performed it in the field. She developed a plan of attack while walking back to the carcass.

The moose had died lying on its right side so she would start skinning and cutting on its left. First, she worked to cut the skin along the back bone from the top of its head to the tail. She made a cut and worked the blade beneath the skin, always working with the blade pointed up to keep the meat as clean as possible. Bending over, she slit the front leg from the hoof to the slit along the animal's back. Next, Elizabeth started to skin the flaps down toward the stomach of the animal. Soon, he front leg was skinless and ready to be separated from the body. However, the limb was too heavy for her to hold up and cut at the same time. She decided to remove the meat from the bone while it was attached to the animal.

She spread the tarp out next to the carcass and started cutting. First, the meat from the lower leg was removed. Next, she began filleting meat from the scapula. With the limb bare, it was significantly lighter, and Elizabeth was able to lift and remove the leg from the carcass. She flopped the leg onto the tarp and saw a significant amount of meat on the back side of the shoulder, which she attacked next.

Elizabeth figured she had worked for over an hour and only had one leg done. She needed a break to give her back a rest and drink some water. She sat back against a rock to rest and drank the steaming water from her mug. Eyeing the half-skinned animal, she wondered how she was going to protect her new-found wealth from both spoilage and bears. Elizabeth closed her eyes for a minute to breathe. She reveled in the knowledge that she had food again.

After her break, she started on the back leg. She worked with renewed vigor and soon had the back leg bare. This one was even heavier than the front. She worked to take large chunks of meat off and lay them on the tarp. At last, she could lift the leg enough to get her knife into the ball socket of the hip. The tendon in the socket was hard to find, but after some digging, there was a loud pop, and the leg moved freely. She transferred the limb to the tarp and continued to remove meat from the femur and lower leg. Soon, there were two naked legs, each attached to its hoof, lying in the grass next to the carcass. Her body ached as she arched her back in a deep stretch while taking a drink of water. She needed to keep going but needed a snack to replenish her energy. She started a fire near the carcass and retrieved her roasting spit as it burnt down to coals. Two pieces of meat were sizzling over the fire as she returned to take the backstrap off of the moose.

Elizabeth struggled with the back meat. The piece of meat ran parallel to the spine, which required her to be on her knees and roll the large piece of meat toward her as she separated the muscle from the bone. The effort produced a log of meat almost as tall as Elizabeth, which she carried over her shoulder like a sack of potatoes.

She checked the skewered meat chunks and rotated them so the other sides were toward the fire. Next, she had to flip the huge animal. A few attempts revealed that it would be impossible to move with its entrails intact. A pile of innards so close to camp made her nervous, but what choice did she have? The moose was dead and it didn't matter if the guts were in or out of the carcass. She went back to camp and found the second tarp, placing it beneath the animal. After a final assessment, Elizabeth made an incision in the soft tissue of the abdomen. The stomachs and coils of intestines burst from the cavity. She tugged and pulled to guide the guts onto the tarp. After numerous grunts and sweat, the entrails were finally laying on the tarp. It had been a bloody, smelly job that made her gag multiple times. Laying the knife on the rib cage, Elizabeth bent down to grab the tarp. She pulled with all her might, but only managed to just budge the tarp. After a rest, she tugged again. This time it started to slide, and she was able to drag it away from both the carcass and the camp.

There was an intoxicating scent from the roasted meat. Golden brown cubes sizzled over the coals with chunks of fat crackling on their edges. After washing her hands in the lake, she used her fingers to remove one of the hunks from the stick and took a bite. The meat was slightly tough and cooked to medium rare. Juices ran down her chin and fingers. She licked her fingers clean after finishing.

Elizabeth reassessed after supper. The sun was sinking below the trees. She needed to get the meat back to a hanging tree before nightfall. She took the game bags and started to stuff the meat inside. She wished she had done this earlier to protect the exposed muscle from insects. She shooed them away before packing up the meat. She had decided to stay up all night to guard her kill from predators. She went back to camp and got as much firewood as possible and then made a second trip. Finally, Elizabeth made a third trip to retrieve her sleeping bag and mat. She built up the fire again to help fight the bugs, which were terrible but usually died down after dusk.

She settled in for the night. Her sleeping bag was in the grass next to an old stump she could lean against. Her rifle was lying next to her with a round chambered and the safety on. Leaning back against the stump caused her to doze, but she fought against sleep with all her might. She knew that bears had an amazing sense of smell, allowing them to detect both blood and guts from miles away. Defending the meat was her job.

Elizabeth's head leaned back against the stump and her eyes fluttered shut. She was sore and the cold crept over her body. The sleeping bag was so warm and she put her nose in her shirt to keep it warm. She was slipping in and out of sleep when crackling twigs caught her attention. She snapped awake and grabbed the rifle in one fluid movement. The night was still as she peered into the inky black beyond the dome of firelight. The silence seemed to press in on her, making her ragged breathing sound loud. Eventually, exhaustion overcame her and she dozed off.

DAY 16

Elizabeth jerked awake at the first grunt. It had come from behind her. She sprang out of her sleeping bag and grabbed her rifle in one swift movement. She ran to the other side of the fire because she wanted to keep the flames between her and whatever was in the woods. She fed the fire with one hand while keeping the gun pointed toward the direction of the noise. The grunts came from the trees, but no movement could be seen.

Fear had controlled her. Her body shook and she found herself screaming to release the tension building in her gut. She hollered, "Hey, bear!" repeatedly just like she had practiced with her dad. Next, she danced around the fire, whooping and hollering while holding the gun over her head to look like she was bigger. Finally, she raised the rifle and flipped the safety off, needing to be ready if the situation arose. She continued to shout, "Hey, bear! Back up bear! Get away, bear!"

The bear did not back down. Woofing sounds continued from the trees and finally it emerged into the clearing. It was standing as a shadow on the edge of the fire's light. The bruin was paced back and forth at the edge of the forest. It paused occasionally to paw at the ground and growl. Elizabeth raised the rifle for a warning shot in the ground in front of the bear. She pulled the trigger and hit just in front of the brute. Debris flew into the bear's face causing it to roar and then retreat into the woods.

Elizabeth's hands finally stopped shaking as the eastern sky started to turn gray. She kept the fire burning the rest of the night and spent her time shouting into the darkness to prevent another close encounter. She hoped that her constant movement would alert the woods to her presence. Exhaustion was setting in as the sun finally crested the trees. She felt that she could finally relax. However, there was still a lot of work to do before the carcass could be abandoned.

Elizabeth decided that she needed some breakfast before starting again so she did her morning chores. She found a trout in the fish trap, which she had neglected to check the night before. She roasted the trout for breakfast and sipped a mug of warm water to help relax and warm up. She stared into the ashy coals of the fire and reflected on the night before. The bear had stayed away after the warning shot. She wasn't sure if it was luck or if she had actually scared the bear. Relaxation settled into her body with the warm water, fire, and food. She began nodding off after finishing breakfast.

She woke up with a start and didn't know where she was. She fumbled for the rifle as she recalled the events of the previous night. She worked the bolt and turned a full circle, scanning the edge of the clearing. Nothing was out of the ordinary. The moose carcass was still by the lake shore. It had transformed from a brown, furry lump to a red and white mass of bone, muscle, and sinew.

Elizabeth grabbed her knife and headed back to the kill site to finish flipping and cleaning the carcass. The body of the animal was much lighter with the entrails removed. She was able to flip it, after repositing the head and using the leverage of its legs. The legs had gone into rigor mortis overnight and the fat was starting to solidify, which made it more difficult to skin the right side of the animal. By noon, she had finished the front leg and was starting to skin back the hide from the hind leg. She was hungry and thirsty.

She found boiled water left over from the night before. Taking a long drink and then a second, she stared at the pile of meat on the tarp. The next step was hanging all of that protein in trees after finishing cleaning the carcass, which needed to be done before going to bed. She was exhausted, both physically and mentally, with no intention of spending another night exposed next to a carcass. She walked to the bear vault to retrieve a couple of granola bars and found the old bear tracks still in the soil.

Elizabeth finished the butchering job by removing the right backstrap of the moose. Her body was resigning itself to fatigue and shook as she crouched to make the final cuts to free the hunk of protein. Standing took all of her effort as she hoisted the large chunk of meat. She slapped it down on the tarp and she rolled onto her back next to the piles on the tarp. Each side of the moose was arranged in a pile. The left side was already in game bags, but the right still needed to be packaged. However, she needed to have a proper lunch before she could do any more work. It was mid-afternoon and the meat needed to be stored before nightfall.

The meat was bagged up and ready to be hung. She had a limited supply of paracord after anchoring the fish trap, so she decided to climb trees to hang the meat. Brown bears don't climb trees as adults so she thought the meat would be safer. Her task was more difficult than she expected. Elizabeth could climb the trees fine by herself, but lugging fifty pounds sacks of meat made it impossible. Finally, she was forced to use a haul line. The paracord was tied to a bag and Elizabeth hooked the other end to a belt loop. She could climb the tree, sit, and then pull the meat up to the branch. She then nestled it in the crook of a tree. She stored the majority of the meat this way and the rest she hung with the remaining paracord for easy access over the next couple days. Meat preservation was the next problem to solve. Smoked meat could be stored, but she was too tired to think about the process.

Elizabeth brought a couple of chunks back to camp for supper. The meat cooked while she did her evening chores. She decided to leave the fish trap until morning. She ate supper, took one more look around camp, and headed to the tent. While stripping her outer layers, she noticed blood caked onto her forearms and dried on her pants and sweater. She decided a bath would be her first item in the morning. The dried blood on her clothes made her nervous, so she slipped her boots back on and jogged to the supply tent in her base layers. Her eyes slammed shut the instant she was zipped into her bag. The sun had not even dipped below the trees.

DAY 17

Elizabeth woke with gray light in her tent once again. She could smell herself, which reminded her that the first order was a bath and laundry after her chores. Her chores went as usual. No fish had been in her trap and the moose meat was as she left it in the trees. Retrieving a bit of the meat from her cache, she headed back to camp to cook breakfast. The mornings had gotten cooler with the passing days. The crash was almost two-and-a-half weeks ago. She thought about all she had been through since that time.

The sun was shining when she emerged from her supply tent with a camp towel, clean clothes, and a small bottle of soap. She went down to the shore and stripped off her base layers to take an invigorating cold-water bath. Diving in caused her to huff and puff in the cold as she washed her hair and body. Blood flaked off her arms as she scrubbed. Once she was clean, dry, and dressed, she set out to do laundry. The learning curve had been steep but now she was a pro; she was done in no time. Her clothes were draped over rocks, drying, and she was warmed up again by mid-morning. Finally, she heated some water and sat down to take a break. The crisp air created a pleasing cloud of steam and the sun warmed her face.

Elizabeth sipped her water while she thought about the next step to process her kill. She needed to preserve the moose meat hanging in the trees. She knew that the pioneers and Native Americans used smoke to preserve meat, but she was pretty sure salt was involved. She was fresh out of salt. Her dad taught her to make jerky and the first step was slicing the meat very thin. Usually, he brined the meat in a spice mix before putting it on the smoker. Making smoke was not a problem, so she decided to try smoking without the spices. She would test her process with a small batch.

First, she found her roasting spits. After a trip to the food cache and her supply tent she was ready to start slicing. The meat was firmer and drier than she thought. She had imagined a slimy mess in the game bags because they had used plastic bags to store meat at home. The cloth game bags had allowed air to flow around the meat and keep it dry. She hoped this would allow the meat to stay fresh longer. Elizabeth had a four-or-five pound chunk of maroon meat on a log that she had wiped down. She started slicing the roast as thin as possible. Slicing was more difficult than she was used to. Her dad always partially froze the venison before making jerky. The fresh meat was hard to cut evenly. After a half an hour, the slicing was complete and resulted in a satisfying pile of meat.

Elizabeth threaded the slices onto her spits, but noticed that the method wouldn't work like the fish. If she set the stick at an angle, the cuts crowded each other and wouldn't cook evenly. She found two Y-shaped sticks and stuck them on either side of the fire pit. Then, she set the spit in the "y's" to create a drying rack. The apparatus looked sturdy enough. Finally, she spaced the pieces of meat so no pieces touched. She set the skewer back on the log while she lit a fire.

She went and grabbed an armful of kindling and logs. Soon, a fire was roaring in the pit. She took a granola bar break and waited for the fire to burn down to coals. She returned with more firewood and finally set the meat over the coals. She went to check the clothes. They were dry, so Elizabeth gathered them and put them back in the supply tent.

The aroma of roasting meat filled her nostrils and she ran to the pit. "Shit!" she yelled as she ran over to the fire. She grabbed the skewer and inspected the meat. The meat was cooking rather than drying. Luckily, it was not burned. She decided to continue cooking the strips then figure out what to do with them. She flipped the spit for even cooking. She added a couple logs to burn down near the ring. The smell was intoxicating, and she was ready for supper when the meat was done roasting. She hadn't caught any fish that day, which was okay.

While eating supper, Elizabeth sat and thought about how to dry the meat on her next attempt. Obviously, there was too much heat and not enough smoke. She needed to reverse the equation. She needed to create more smoke from the coals, but how? She completed her evening chores. She stuck the cooled meat into an extra game bag and put it in the game vault.

She went to bed that night thinking about the smoke problem, which caused her to dream about fires.

She was observing a wildfire from a distance. The fire was moving through a stand of beetle-killed trees. The fire hit a stand of green wood and the whole scene changed. Suddenly, there was a great plume of white smoke. The dream ended as she flew away from the flames. She woke up with an idea of how to make a cool, smoky fire.

DAY 18

Thunder woke Elizabeth the next morning. Not booming crashes that remind one of the apocalypse, but rather the lazy, rolling thunder of a calm fall storm trolling by. Lightning lit the sky through the tent, but it created a calming effect. Soon, rain started to patter against the tarp of the tent. The sound was relaxing and Elizabeth laid back to listen to the music. She drifted off again with an idea of drying meat.

Elizabeth woke again to the rain falling against the tarp. There was a popping noise with each impact. The drops were falling perpendicular to the tarp. She watched the water trails careen down the side of the tent. The gray light highlighted the droplets against the green tarp. She stayed in her sleeping bag as long as she could. Her bladder eventually drove her to dress and meet the ducky day. She looked around and realized that there was no hope of building a drying fire.

She checked the trap and found two large trout. They were quickly dispatched and she lit the camp stove from the supply tent. The steam started to rise from the pot before the water boiled. She slipped a trout into the pan to poach. Nibbling a granola bar, she poked her head out of the tent. The sky was a steely gray without a speck of blue in sight. There was not much to do until the rain eased. She decided it would be a day of rest. The poached fish were delicious, and she cleaned up after breakfast.

Running back and forth to the supply tent got her clothes soaked. She stripped down to her base layers and dried her hair with a camp towel. Finally, she crawled back into the sleeping bag to relax, which gave her a rare moment for reflection. Elizabeth had spent so much time focusing on survival that she had not processed all that had happened since the crash. Questions arose in her mind. What had her parents been doing? How many days had it been? She was pretty sure it had been seventeen days since the crash.

Her spirits dipped as she thought about the hell her parents had been experiencing. She had not been away for more than a long weekend in eighteen years. The plane crash had driven an insurmountable chasm between them, removing all communication. Her eyes welled when she thought of her parents getting the news. How long had her dad waited until he found out her plane was missing? What was the phone call to her mom like? Were they in Alaska?

A thought struck Elizabeth like a bolt of lightning. How much longer would the search and rescue last? Panic rose in her stomach at the sudden realization that the search would be called off if she wasn't found soon. The fall rescue mission would turn to a spring recovery mission because she did not have the gear to survive an Alaskan winter. A tingling sensation radiated from her abdomen to her chest then spread to her limbs as panic swelled in her body. A lump rose in her throat as panic waxed for a final assault.

The feeling erupted as body wrenching sobs, and her face twisted in a painful grimace. The sobs made her feel out of control and her breathing became ragged. The waves rolled over her again and again until she felt like she was drowning; she just couldn't stop. She would calm down for a moment before the fear returned and the whole process started over again. Eventually, her body couldn't produce any more tears. Her body ached from the full body tremors and panic attacks. Her breathing came under control, and exhaustion swept over her body. Burying her head in her make-shift pillow, she closed her eyes for some rest.

Elizabeth awoke more relaxed but the panic was bubbling just under the surface. After a few moments, she realized that the world was quieter than it had been before. The light filtering into the tent was yellow and more intense than earlier. She sat up wrapped in her sleeping bag and stretched her arms. Action was her only path forward. She needed to refuel her body and remembered the strips of cooked moose meat.

She made a meal of boiled meat in broth. She sat and sipped as the sun slipped toward the western horizon. She had accomplished almost nothing on the soggy day. Nevertheless, she had realized that there needed to be more action if she was going to be rescued. First, she needed to cook breakfast in the morning, and then make a drying fire. This time there would be plenty of wet wood to make it smoke. Elizabeth wanted to have a good supply of wood for the morning and headed for the log pile by the lake. The forest was damp everywhere. She picked the smallest pieces to bring back to camp. The sticks were stacked to increase airflow. She hoped they would be dry by noon to try her drying fire. Elizabeth went to bed that night with less anxiety. She had resolved to be found, which gave her a new purpose. She curled into her sleeping bag and shifted until she was comfortable. Her mom and dad popped into her mind again. She knew they were working tirelessly with the rescue effort, not sitting back and letting the authorities handle her disappearance. Survival was necessary, so her suffering wouldn't be in vain. A fighting spirit awoke in her body. She drifted off to sleep resolving that the woods wouldn't conquer her.

DAY 19

The day came bright and clean with the birds calling in the trees and the golden light reflecting off the water. Elizabeth prepared for the day and started her chores. There were fish in the trap, which she cleaned for breakfast. The trap was reset using fish entrails for bait. Next, she checked the firewood pile for dry fuel. Some of the wood appeared dry enough to use but would not stay lit in her firepit. She poached the fish on the camp stove for a second day. The flesh peeled easily from the bones, and she drank the flavorful poaching liquid from the aluminum pot.

She went back to the meat trees to check the game bags after the rain. She took one down and inspected it. Everything was still smelling fresh, but she was appalled when she opened it up. The meat was a sickly gray color. She took out a chunk and smelled it. There was no off-putting smell, but it looked like meat that had been in the fridge for too long. Repacking the meat, Elizabeth bundled the bag and took it back to camp. The morning was spent slicing the meat from the bag while she waited for the firewood to dry. She also needed some green wood to help create smoke, but she wasn't sure what type of wood to use. Her dad used hickory, oak, and apple at home but there were none of those trees around up here. Maybe willows would work, but they were so far away.

At camp, Elizabeth sat down with her knife to work on slicing the cuts of meat. She decided that she would need to get as much done as possible in the next few days to prevent spoilage. Slicing was easier on her second attempt. Before she knew it, there was a pile of sliced meat, which she packed in her game bags before taking a break for lunch.

After eating some boiled moose strips for lunch, Elizabeth tried to light a fire again. The flames stayed alive in some bark strips and she slowly fed larger pieces until there was a large fire ripping in the pit. Next, she threaded the meat strips on the skewers as the fire burned down to coals. She did not want to walk all the way to the willows so she went to the nearest pine tree with a small hand saw from the equipment tent. Within a few minutes, she had cut a pile of pine boughs. She bundled the branches in her arms and carried them back to the fire.

The fire was nearly down to coals, so she put a green branch on top of the bed of embers. The first branch dried up and burned rapidly, so she added two more. The second batch gave off a respectable amount of smoke, which gave Elizabeth a chance to lay the meat over the posts. The smoke curled up and around the strips of meat as she tended the fire all day. The lack of activity gave her plenty of time to think. She thought about how she could signal the rescuers from her location. The signal fire was sitting undisturbed but wet from the day before. The pile of sticks was relatively large compared to her campfire, and it probably could send up enough smoke to be seen for miles. If there happened to be a plane close it would work, but it was useless to her if the plane was miles away.

How could she signal? She was truly in the middle of nowhere. Everyone joked back home that Bismarck was in the middle of nowhere, but there was a Sam's Club and Costco, along with dozens of restaurants. The Alaskan wilderness, however, was literally hundreds of miles away from the nearest road. She remembered something from a documentary. A group of hikers had started a forest fire to signal their location. Would that work in such a remote area? Fires were probably allowed to burn themselves out so far away from homes or infrastructure.

The afternoon passed and the pile of wood and green boughs shrank. The meat appeared to be done. It had gone from a wet and raw to the deep maroon color of smoked meat. Elizabeth broke a piece off the end of a slice and popped it in her mouth. A strong pine flavor assaulted her taste buds as she chewed the chunk of meat, which, combined with the lack of salt, was different from what they made at home. She spat out the chunk and looked at the rack of dried meat in frustration. The pine boughs had tainted the whole batch. She couldn't throw the meat out though, so she packed it in a freshly laundered game bag before storing it in the food vault. The food wouldn't go to waste, but she decided to eat the roasted leftovers first.

The sunset that night was particularly beautiful. Oranges mixed with pinks and reds in the western sky to light the tops of the trees. The light show was better than any firework show Elizabeth had ever witnessed. She cleaned up and then proceeded to do her evening chores. She stacked some extra wood for the next morning before heading to her tent. She drifted to sleep thinking about the sunset and picturing the color burst in her mind's eye.

She dreamt that night. It was not particularly scary, but it was foreboding. She seemed to float above camp. Winter had set in and the forest was covered in a blanket of snow. There was a trail of packed snow to the food vault and around camp. However, it was impossible to haul wood from the frozen lake. Elizabeth floated to the tent and saw through the tarp. There was a girl wrapped in all her gear shivering in her sleeping bag. It was an unpleasant experience, but she couldn't wake herself.

The dream proceeded through the Alaskan winter. First, the girl was able to spud through the thin ice for water to boil with the camp stove. Next, she saw her eating chunks of frozen meat because she had run out of fuel for the stove and had no access to dry firewood. Finally, she was floating over camp looking at the tent and surrounding area. A blanket of fresh snow was spread around camp, but there were no signs of any human activity. The sun was low in the sky but standing straight south, indicating it was noon. Elizabeth hovered outside the tent, hesitant to enter. She was afraid of what she would find inside. She closed her eyes and willed herself to wake up. The dream ended, as she felt herself float into the steely winter sky. She opened her eyes one last time and saw the tent become a point of black in the white landscape.

DAY 20

The day was clear and bright when Elizabeth woke the next morning. Her dream emphasised the dire need for rescue. It was the middle of September and there could be snow at any time. Her dad had specifically scheduled the trip before the typical first snow fall, but that time was starting to pass. Elizabeth lay in her sleeping bag longer than normal thinking about how to signal for help.

She worked up the courage to get up and face the day. Her chores were capped with a couple of fish in the trap, which were cleaned and the trap reset. Next, she sat down to start the fire so she could cook her meal. It was going to be another experimental day. She would work on trying to find the right wood to smoke the moose meat. Elizabeth thought she would try willow this time. The fire was almost down to coals so she spitted the fish and set them to roast, when a grunting alerted her to the woods.

Elizabeth's head snapped to the tree line to see the bear coming out of the woods toward the gut pile. The pile was putrified after five days in the sun. The bear huffed and released a low growl as it walked across the clearing. It got to the pile in no time and stood next to the pile grunting in her direction, while she stood slack jawed and reached for her rifle. The bolt slowly slipped a fresh cartridge into the chamber. Meanwhile, the bruin had started to dig its face into the pile. It was eating like the offal was life-saving, which, with hibernation coming, it probably was. The bear exposed fresh tissue in the pile. Teeth ripped through the soft, desiccated intestines and claws dug into the pile to pull his next bite into position.

Elizabeth felt that the bear would leave her alone while the gut pile lasted, but she didn't want to get into a territorial battle with this giant over the meat. The bear would obviously annihilate her mano a mano. She decided to try to scare the bruin away with a warning shot. Raising the scope to her eye, she aimed for the ground just to the side of the bear. The rifle blast disturbed the forest's silence. The bear jumped and grunted then started its retreat from the noise and exploding soil. It galloped toward the trees at an impressive pace, as its brown backside disappeared into the bushes. Working the bolt, she replaced the empty with a fresh round and picked up the spent casing. The forest was quiet again, but, soon, birds started to sing in the trees.

The fish were ready before she knew it. Eating, Elizabeth realized that she needed to take another trip to the willows, which made her nervous after her recent encounters. Bears were essentially invisible in the forest. "How long will a bear stay away after a loud noise?" she wondered aloud. She would have to be careful and walk with her rifle at the ready. She finished breakfast then added some logs to the fire to ensure there would be coals when she returned.

Gathering wood had taken more time than she expected. Elizabeth struggled to fell the thin, whippy trees. Further, it took time removing the leaves from the limbs because there was too much moisture. By the time she was finished, there were ten poles bundled and ready when she was done. Each pole was long and would need to be cut down being added to the fire. The trip back to camp was difficult with lots of stumbling and the bundle snagging on everything. It was after lunch by the time Elizabeth returned to camp. The coals were almost out. She added some wood and ate while the new fuel burned down. After eating a granola bar, she cut the willow sticks. Finally, she was ready to string the meat on the skewers again.

Fragrant smoke filled the air as she sat back and admired the new apparatus. Whisps of willow smoke bathed the strips hanging from the skewers. The fire had a different smell from the hardwood fires at home, but it did not smell piney. Leaving the fire, she went to the fishing rock to rest for a bit.

Elizabeth sat on the rock looking out at the lake. A twinge of anxiety settled in her stomach at the sudden thought of not being found. She felt a pity party brewing, which would not help her get rescued. "What am I going to do?" played on repeat in her mind. She had no connection to the outside world. She couldn't walk to any roads, because she had no idea which direction to start. She couldn't follow the stream because the woods were too thick. There were no options. "Would a daily signal fire work?" she said aloud. It was a gamble because it would burn precious fuel that she would need if it got cold. She weighed the decision for a while and decided to start the signal fire the next day. She stood to head back to the camp after.

The wet wood was down to coals when she returned to the fire. She spent the rest of the afternoon feeding fresh willow sticks to the coal bed. In between, Elizabeth made extra trips to the wood pile for fuel. She even made one more trip to the willow patch for more green wood. Finally, the meat had the deep maroon look of preserved meat.

Elizabeth tore off a piece from one of the strips of muscle. The meat had white fibers between the strands like the jerky her dad made at home. She put a small piece in her mouth and chewed. The meat tasted better from the pine-smoked meat from the previous day. It had a lighter taste that lingered on her tongue after she swallowed. The taste was fresh and finished with a slight lingering bitterness. It was delicious and she polished off three more pieces for supper. She packed the rest of the meat into the game bag in the bear vault.

Elizabeth needed many days of smoking meat to finish processing the whole moose. "But it's not like I don't have them," she said as she walked back to camp. She turned and saw smoke rising in the sinking sun. Her little fire was producing a visible column of smoke, which spurred an idea. Her cooking fires would work as a signal as well. She could build several smoking fires and do multiple batches of meat at the one time. This meant making more skewers and stands, but she could make them in the morning.

Elizabeth went to bed that night thinking about her new plan. It would be a busy morning, but she should be able to get everything ready in a few hours. Her sleep was uninterrupted.

DAY 21

Elizabeth was awake before the dawn broke the next morning. She had lots to prepare if she was going accomplish her goal. It was ambitious, but she was ready. She went over her to-do list as she ate some moose jerky for breakfast. First, she needed more dry wood from the lakeshore. Next, she made more skewers and racks. She planned on having four fires going, each with two skewers, which meant she needed to make six more sets. Then, she would spend the afternoon transporting willow sticks to camp. At last, she was ready to start.

She spent two or three hours stocking the wood supply. Elizabth made sure that she took all of the top dry material first, then she started to gather some of the partially submerged branches. She made different piles. One with dry and another with wet. She hoped the wood would dry out by the time she needed it. She spent the next couple of hours making six sets of skewers and racks. The sun was overhead by the time she was done, so she made some lunch.

Next, she made multiple excursions to get as many willow branches as she could. Her trail became more established with each pass, making each trip slightly easier than the last. She had fifty sticks, which was enough for a few days. She planned to gather ten more each day after the fires were lit and smoking. She figured she could make it back to camp before the fires burned down too much.

Finally, Elizabeth worked on cutting the meat for the next day, which took her until evening. She had made a schedule for her preservation days. She planned to prepare for the next day while the meat was smoking. Each morning would begin by starting the fires, which would burn down to coals during morning chores. Next, she would load the meat onto skewers. She would put the skewers on the racks then add willow chunks to each. Then, she would start prepping for the next day by cutting meat, cutting willow sticks, and gathering wood. The meat would be done in the evening and she could make supper. Following this plan, she hoped to preserve all of the moose meat in five or six days.

The day had been productive, and Elizabeth was ready for her "factory" to start in the morning. She went to bed and had another dreamless night. Just as she was starting to drift off, she worried that the fire would not produce enough smoke to signal planes. But she let this thought go, and drifted off into a deep slumber.

DAY 22

The process of smoking meat was well underway by the middle of the next morning. The fire had been easy to start and she had loaded the meat on the skewers faster than she planned. She was surprised by how much smoke the fires generated. Together, the fires were significantly larger than any of the other fires she had started. There was a large column of smoke rising above the tree tops. It was likely a passing plane would catch a glimpse of the plume and investigate her camp-site.

Her chores were neglected from the day before, so Elizabeth had some work to do getting camp back into shape. The fish trap held two fish, which were cleaned and roasted over one of the fires. The kitchen was cleaned up by the time the fish were ready, and she had a hardy lunch and reflected on her morning.

She was proud of her accomplishments in the woods. All of that work would pay off when she saw her family again. Focusing on survival had driven home the importance of self-reliance. Problem solving day-to-day was an important skill in both the wilderness and life in general. Elizabeth wouldn't give up and couldn't afford mistakes. Out here, consequences for her decisions were life and death; yet, she liked this new responsibility. It was freeing. There was a touch of rebellion in her new-found independence.

She kept looking forward to the next steps. Planning for the future was important, but so was improvising when things did not go as planned. Elizabeth felt a fire to survive burning in her belly. It would have been easy to sit in the tent and starve after the camp food ran out. "Do hard things," was what her dad said. The phrase had not made sense until now. There is always a hard part of life, but those are the parts worth doing.

The beauty around camp was starting to feel like a home. The trees of the clearing were her walls, grass and rocks the floor, and the blue sky her ceiling. Light was either the sun itself or fire derived from wood that the sun had nurtured. Nature provided Elizabeth's food through fish, a bird, and now a moose. At home, food still came from the grocery store, even though she had grown up in an agricultural state. Additionally, hunting was part of Elizabeth's life in North Dakota, but she never expected to be reliant on it. She was taking a graduate course in living off the land and she was excelling. Pride swelled in her chest, and she felt like a grownup.

After lunch, she collected firewood, gathered willow trunks, and cut up moose meat. Elizabeth prepped for the next day all afternoon. By the end of the day, two whole bags of moose meat were preserved. None of the meat had rotted. There had been a few slimy spots, but she cut them off like her mom had done. She had two or three days more work to finish smoking the meat.

Supper that evening was smoked moose meat. She

was going to bed that night when she looked back at the carcass. There was something different about the gut pile. She loaded a round into the rifle and walked over to the carcass. Elizabeth noticed two things as she approached the pile. First, the pile was significantly smaller than it was before. There was only a bit of greenish pink intestine laying around. The stomach tissue had been consumed and the contents were left looking like a pile of lawn clippings. Second, there were signs of bears all around. Tracks had been back and forth to the woods multiple times. The grass was beat down into a path from all the traffic. The bear must have been visiting at night while she slept.

Elizabeth jumped up and instantly looked at the woods where the trail disappeared into the forest. She felt an urge to run but didn't want to be pursued. She held the rifle over her head and slowly walked backward toward camp. She went into her tent and zipped it shut. Going to sleep that night was almost impossible. She jumped and readied the gun at any sound. Sleep finally came, but it was restless.

Sometime just before dawn, she heard grunting as the bear worked on reducing the pile of viscera to nothing. Elizabeth got out of bed and quietly unzipped her tent, poking her head out into the darkness. The moonless sky was inky black with pinpricks of stars, which reflected off the mirror smooth lake. The wind had died down; it was a cold night. The only disturbance was the grunting and chewing of the bear across the clearing. She stared into the pitch black willing herself to see the shape of the invisible bruin. She stood and stepped out of the tent, barefoot and in her base layers. The ground was icy cold on her bare feet, causing a dull ache in her soles.

Raising the rifle to her shoulder, she pointed it in the direction of the noises. She slipped the safety forward and placed her finger on the trigger. The rifle explosion felt rude to the cold peace of the forest. The blast scared her and Elizabeth fumbled with the bolt to load another cartridge. She realized that she could hear the bear retreating into the woods. Its large feet were padding the soft ground and its panting filled the air. She stood watch outside her tent in the darkness ready for anything.

The cold ground eventually pushed her back into the tent. The rifle lay next to her as she lay in her sleeping bag shivering from both fear and cold. Two thoughts were running through her mind simultaneously. First, this would not be the last visit from the bear. Second, the nights were getting colder. Snow would come any day. She drifted off into an uneasy but dreamless sleep.

DAY 23

Elizabeth woke before first light and witnessed the sunrise in a cloudless sky. Colors burst from the east as the sun emerged over the horizon. She distracted herself from the bear by finishing morning chores and eating a breakfast of moose meat. Next, she worked on getting the meat skewered onto the sticks while the smoking fire burned down to coals. The air was colder than it had been the rest of the trip. She didn't give it a second thought, but did put on another layer from the supply tent while waiting for the fire to burn down to coals.

She placed the skewers on the rack, then spaced the meat out before placing green willow trunks on the coals. The smoke was just starting to curl off the green wood when the wind came up. The tops of the trees started to sway with the gusts. She looked around camp and realized the western horizon was steely blue. The wind swirled in the clearing, making it hard to tell which way the wind was blowing. A storm was brewing. Elizabeth zipped up her outer coat, dug a beanie out of her pocket, and pulled it over her ears. Next, she found a pair of gloves and slipped them on. She was already feeling warmer, but she was nervous about sleeping in a tent through a storm. The temp had dropped further by the time the coals were ready for a second batch of willow.

Her ears perked up as the smoke curled over the meat. The shaking trees were making it hard to distinguish, but there was an unnatural sound on the breeze. She held her breath and moved her head to focus on the sound. A low, steady buzz was definitely coming from the sky. She realized it was an engine and, more importantly, it was getting louder. Her heart leapt into her chest as she realized a plane was coming.

She rushed to her fires and tossed on all the wood she had. Then, she ran to the signal fire while retrieving the lighter she had kept in her pocket. She stuck her hand into the log-cabin pile and flicked the lighter three times. It wouldn't light; there was too much wind. Elizabeth paused, closed her eyes, and took a few long deep breaths. She could hear the plane getting closer to the camp. She wanted the fire to be burning by the time the plane flew over. Finally, she realized there were already fires burning. She ran to grab a long stick with a glowing end from the smoking fire and brought it over to the signal pyre. She thrust the glowing end into the kindling and held it there. Soon, it was smoking and suddenly burst into flames. The small tongues of flame in the kindling began licking at the large pile of wood, causing smoke to rise from the structure. Eventually, the logs caught and the whole structure was blazing. A big, hot fire was raging from her makeshift firepit.

Her focus went back to the sky. The drone of the engine was unmistakable. It was overpowering the wind. It was so close that it felt like the plane should be on top of her. Hope surged in her chest as she scanned the sky, waiting for the plane to pop over the trees. The noise was all she could hear. A chilling thought came that it might be an auditory mirage or she was dreaming. She swallowed hard to bury the thought. Seconds crawled by as her anticipation built.

The plane seemed to explode over the treetops. It was white and green, with a single engine and floats to land on the water. The plane was traveling north to south. Elizabeth ran along the shoreline waving her hands as the plane flew over the lake. She thought for a moment that it was going to keep going, but, at the last minute, it banked hard over the forest. Tears rolled down her face as the plane set a course directly back to her camp. It waggled its wings as it flew over the lake. The pilot had seen the camp and was signaling to her. She was saved! Sobs came wrenching out of her body as the stress of the past three weeks erupted in a slew of emotions. Relief came like a blanket until she looked at the lake.

Large waves were rolling from the high winds. Moments later, wind-driven snowflakes hit her face. What did this mean for the plane? She found the plane again as it lined itself up for a landing approach to the lake. It made a pass then banked around for a second go. It was out of sight for a moment before coming over the trees at a crawl. It was losing altitude, but right before the floats hit the water the pilot hit the throttle and pulled the nose up. She watched in horror as the plane made one more pass then headed back the way it had come.

She screamed for the plane to come back as it disappeared over the trees and out of sight. She was so close. She had to wait for the weather to clear. It was all too much. Elizabeth went back to the tent and lay down. She cried herself to sleep; forgetting about the racks of meat drying near the fire.

She woke up many hours later. Disappointment lingered in her stomach, but hope was shining through. The plane knew where she was and she would be rescued. She opened her tent to a landscape of green and white. The snow had continued and accumulated to blanket the ground. Her boots crunched as she made her way toward the fire. The bed of coals was cold. There was snow collecting on the cold meat. She doubted if she could get another fire going today, but she gave it a try anyway.

She went to the wood pile and dug into the dry wood in the middle. She was able to rekindle the fire, but she did not want to overcook the meat again. She moved the racks of red muscle to the rocks while the fire burned down to coals. She took the opportunity to warm up while gazing into the fire as it danced up the dry wood. There was a quiet about the woods as snow started falling again. She could almost hear the soft flakes hitting the ground, which caused a hush to fall over the camp. The woods were quiet, and the wind had died as the front moved past.

The serenity was broken by thumping feet and grunting. Elizabeth turned to see a brown mass galloping toward her. The rifle was slung on her shoulder and she swung it off a moment too late. The bear slammed into her and knocked her to the ground. He was on top of her before she knew it.

She tried to go limp like her training, but she found it difficult with the animal's teeth and claws ripping at her flesh. Claws tore through the left sleeve of her coat. A warm sensation crept down her arm, which she assumed was blood flowing from her shoulder. Next, the bear bit her right arm with a crushing force. Pain shot through her like lightning as she cried out before passing out a moment later.

She awoke screaming pain. It shot through her right arm when she tried to get up. She fell back to the ground and moaned as more pain erupted in her shoulder. First, she inspected herself. She couldn't sit up, so she lifted her head to investigate. She could move her right arm easier, but saw that there was blood covering the arm from the elbow down. Elizabeth had trouble moving her left arm and observed a large rip on her jacket. She lifted her head slightly to look around camp, but there was no sign of the bruin. She picked her head up a little more and surveyed what she could. Her tents were undisturbed, which was lucky. Next, she looked at the meat racks. All were smashed to splinters and the meat was gone. But busted skewers were the least of her worries.

Standing was difficult. It hurt to move her arms at all, but her left was worse since it was a shoulder injury. She leaned onto her right elbow and sort of rolled herself up groaning through the jolt of pain that ripped through her upper body. She stood and wobbled once before gaining her balance.

Elizabeth started for the supply tent, which held the first-aid kit. The wounds needed to be cleaned. She knew the bear's teeth were full of bacteria that would cause an infection if untreated. She was banking on getting the antibiotic ointment onto her wounds to prevent infection. As she moved toward the tent, Elizabeth noticed a limp in her left leg. The pain in her arms had distracted her from any lower body injury and she found tenderness in her right thigh.

Finally, she reached the tent. She sat down inside and first worked to remove her outer layers. It was hard work, and she took many breaks so the pain would ease. The right arm was okay to get out of her sleeve, but the left was really painful as the clothing came off the shoulder. She looked at the shoulder and saw it had a deep scratch. She could move her hand and elbow, but her shoulder wound hurt when she moved. She moved her attention to the other arm. Her right forearm had four deep holes in it from the bear's teeth. She needed to get those cleaned ASAP.

Elizabeth applied ointment and bandages to her right arm as best as possible since her left shoulder didn't work well. All the wounds got a dose of antibiotic ointment and large bandages were placed over the areas as best she could. The left arm was a little easier since her whole right arm worked. However, it was still painful to move and it took time. Elizabeth made a sling out of a t-shirt and hung it over her neck to support her injured shoulder. Next, she inspected her right thigh. It had a bruise but nothing was cut. She would just have to live with the pain. She found two bottles of medicine, which she stuck in her pocket. Finally, she extended a trekking pole, which helped her stand. She needed her gun if she was going to sleep.

The light was fading as she made her way back to the attack site. She used the trekking pole as a cane, which helped her move more steadily over the slippery snow. She picked up the gun and inspected it. The scope lenses were packed with snow, along with the muzzle. She would have to clean it before it could be fired.

Exhaustion was setting in, but Elizabeth needed to fix the rifle before going to sleep. She went back to the sleeping tent and eased herself to the ground. After some moaning and groaning from the pain, she lowered herself to a sitting position. After unloading the gun, she pulled the bolt out of the back of the receiver. She looked down the barrel from the back, but there was no light coming through the business end. She tried to dig the plug out with her fingers, but the opening was too small. Finally, she stuck the muzzle under her right arm to melt the snow out. A cold, tingly feeling ran down her arm as the snow started to melt. She turned the gun upside down causing a small slug of snow to hit the tent floor. The barrel was free of obstruction. She reassembled the bolt and fed five cartridges into the magazine. Finally, she closed the bolt with a live round in the chamber, just in case.

She took the pill bottles from her pocket. She shook out two acetaminophen for the pain. The other bottle was Benadryl, which she took as a sleep aid. All three went down in a single slug from her water bottle. Finally, she slipped into her sleeping bag, laying down carefully. Planes and bears were running through her head. She would be in a warm, safe bed tomorrow. She shut her eyes and slept.

DAY 24

Elizabeth awoke to pain shooting through her right arm. The wound was throbbing and she moaned as she sat up. The pain peaked as she sat and looked around the tent for the bottle of acetaminophen she had brought last night. The bottle was under her sleeping mat, and she struggled to open the childproof bottle with two injured arms. The lid finally popped off and pills went flying across the tent. Eliabeth swore as the pills hit the floor. Tears welled up in her eyes from pain and frustration. She picked up two pills and popped them in her mouth. She swallowed the pills with the last of her water and lay back while the medicine took effect.

Elizabeth was thirsty and needed more water. The pain eased from a throbbing presence to a dull ache. She climbed to her feet with the help of the trekking pole and unzipped the tent door. She looked out into a world of white. It was the first blizzard of the season. She had not noticed the muffled flapping of the tent through her pain. A large drift had formed on the windward side of her tent, which blocked some of the wind. The clearing was covered in a layer of snow, and the lake was a dark blob in the white landscape. There was no need to attempt a fire today. However, she needed to leave the tent to go to the bathroom and collect supplies from the other tent.

Elizabeth struggled to dress herself with the injuries. Eventually, she managed to make it out into the storm. She made it to the supply tent to grab the camp stove, which she could use to melt snow to drink. The food cache, however, was too far away. She would have to be content with water for the day. Melting water with the stove helped warm the tent, but she only allowed herself to do that a few times. Conserving fuel to cook for later might be important. She spent the cold, monotonous day bundled in her sleeping bag sipping warm water.

Her shoulder was feeling better, but the right arm was starting to feel hot. She grabbed the first-aid kit that morning and decided it was time to switch bandages. Elizabeth took another dose of acetaminophen and then lit the stove to boil some water. She figured she could boil and cool the water to clean the wound while the medicine kicked in. After an half hour, she took her outer layers off and unwrapped the bandages around her wounded arm. The wound looked worse than the day before. The four punctures were now surrounded by red inflamed skin, which was hot to the touch. The skin around the wounds was hard, like a huge mosquito bite. She cleaned the skin around the wounds with a piece of t-shirt soaked in the boiled water. Next, she tried to clean the wounds themselves, but this was too painful and brought tears to her eyes. She finished by applying more antibiotic ointment and reapplied the bandages. She re-dressed in her layers then curled into the sleeping bag to take a nap.

Elizabeth woke up hungry and thirsty. She checked the conditions while she filled the camp stove pot with snow. The view of the clearing was still obstructed by the falling and blowing snow. Food was not an option, but she could warm up with some melted snow. The small camp stove hissed alive. The snow melted and she added more chunks of snow to the warm water already in the pot. The small flame warmed the tent, but it was short-lived. She sat and sipped steaming water from the pan. Pain had returned to her arms. There was no way to know how long ago she had taken the pain killer. The bottle warned against taking too much to avoid liver damage. The last thing she needed was another emergency. Elizabeth decided to wait until sundown to take another dose. She sat wrapped in her sleeping bag and tried to distract herself as best she could. Sleeping was out of the question due to the pain in her arms. The hours drug on through the day.

By the time the sky started to turn dark, hunger pangs were starting to become intense. She had made it through the long day. She took the final dose of pills and made one more batch of water before going to bed. She knew the plane would be back, but she needed to hold out long enough for the storm to pass. She drank the last of the warm water, curled into her sleeping bag fully clothed, and closed her eyes. Sleep came eventually for another cold night in the tent.

DAY 25

Elizabeth woke up feeling terrible. Exhaustion weighed on her like she had not slept at all. Carefully moving her left hand to her bandaged arm, she could feel the heat of her wound through the bandage. Infection was setting in and she didn't have antibiotics. She sat up, opened the bottle of pain killers, and took two more with the remaining water in her mug. More snow was needed, but standing felt impossible due to her weakness. She rested for a minute after standing with help from the trekking pole. The zipper to the tent took her whole effort, but finally she was able to look out onto her clearing. The sky was a steely gray with enough wind to make choppy waves on the lake. The snow was an even blanket with grass tops sticking out of it like hair. It would be difficult to get to the supply tent, much less the food vault.

She filled the pot of the camp stove with snow and went back into the tent. She started the stove and melted some more snow. She sat and waited for her pain to ease while the water heated. She needed to change the dressings again. The water was cooled enough in about half an hour. She unwrapped the bandages from her right arm. The wounds were now full of puss and the skin around them was hotter, redder, and more inflamed. The wounds looked angry. However, what scared her most was a line of red radiating away from the wound. This was turning into a real emergency and the weather would still prevent a plane from landing. She cleaned the arm as best she could with the water and another t-shirt. Finally, she applied the last tube of antibiotic ointment.

She lay down to try to sleep for the rest of the day. Fitful sleep made the day crawl. The pain and discomfort from the infection caused her to toss and turn. A headache developed and Elizabeth was chilled and sweating from the fever. Vivid dreams of a bear woofing around her tent startled her awake multiple times. Screaming, she would wake up to the hallucination of claws scraping the tent, only to find it was the wind. Then, she would lay in her bag waiting for the bear to come and finish her off. She tried to use breathing techniques to regain control of her anxiety, but she usually ended up crying herself to sleep.

The light finally started to fade. Being trapped by weather and sickness had made the day move at a snail's pace. She had sipped water when she could, but she had run out again. She took time to make one last pot of hot water. Elizabeth didn't bother cleaning the wound again because she wanted to keep the bandages for the next day. She could see the red moving up toward her elbow and knew that the infection was spreading. She used the warm water to take another dose of acetaminophen and then settled in for another long, cold night. She lay shivering in her sleeping bag. She wasn't sure if she was cold or had fever chills, which had gotten worse. Finally, the discomfort eased enough for her to nod off for the night.

DAY 26

Elizabeth had a restless night. She was burning up and the hallucinations of the bear continued into the night. Sleep was not deep nor restive. She was still exhausted the next morning. Her weariness was so complete that she could not stand, and could only crawl. Additionally, she was having trouble identifying reality from hallucination. Her fever was as bad as ever causing her to shiver uncontrollably. She was starving but couldn't access any of her food supplies. The red streak was moving to her bicep and a putrid smell was emanating from the bandage. She knew that if the plane did not come soon, they would find only her body. She did crawl out, grab some snow, and take another dose of pain reliever after the snow melted in her mouth.

The pain was too severe for over-the-counter medication and her arm throbbed continually. She had slipped in and out of consciousness, which made estimating the time since her last dose of meds impossible. Each time she woke up the situation seemed worse.

At last, Elizabeth woke up with a burst of energy. She crawled around and found her notebook near the first-aid kit. She felt that she would not live through the night and wrote a farewell letter to her parents. It read:

Mom and Dad:

I love you both more than anything in the world. I was doing my best to survive and see you again, but I was attacked by a bear the same evening that I saw a plane. I tried to clean the wounds but the bite was infected by the second day.

Mom, I want you to know that all you did for me over the past 18 years is appreciated. I know that you sacrificed yourself so I could pursue my dreams.

Dad, I want you to know that I survived this long because of the lessons and skills you taught me. I hope to get to see everyone again, but wanted to say I love you one last time in case I do not survive.

I love you both!

Elizabeth

She stuffed the note into her pant's pocket and tried to find the pill bottle. She didn't worry about another dose of medicine, but she didn't have any water. She got a final handful of snow to melt in her mouth. She prayed and rolled over in her sleeping bag.

❈ ❈ ❈

She woke to the sound of blades beating against the air and was surprised to see that the sky was still light. The tent swayed and shook with the gusts of the blades as the chopper came in to land. The tent door opened a few moments later. Her dad's head poked through the door. She was barely alert, but she smiled when she saw his face.

EPILOGUE

Nine Months Later:

The remainder of the day she was rescued was a blur. Paramedics had come in after her dad, but Elizabeth had no memory of what happened. She didn't learn the whole story until she woke up in the hospital over a week later. She was missing her right arm from the shoulder down. The infection was at her bicep by the time she reached the hospital and it was too late to save her arm. She was rushed into emergency surgery and it was amputated.

The doctors had told her parents that the operation had saved her life, but she still had a long row to hoe. After the long fever, she had been severely dehydrated. Her mom and dad took shifts sitting with her until she woke seven days later. Her dad was there reading when she had whispered her first words, "I love you, Dad." He jumped up and started crying as he looked into her tired eyes for the first time in almost a month. She remained in the hospital for another month. Elizabeth was walking again after a week. The rest of the time was spent regaining the strength she lost after the infection. The semester was half-way over by the time she was back home. Given the circumstances, however, her spot was held for a year until she made a full recovery.

Winter was tough. Through occupational therapy, she continued learning to live with only one arm. She worked hard during the day then passed out at bedtime. Her social life was back to normal by Christmas, when her friends returned from their first semesters away. January and February saw her making gains by leaps and bounds.

Throughout her therapy, Elizabeth looked to the moose skull for strength. A second chopper had been sent by the Alaskan troopers to investigate the scene. The meat and skull had been recovered as part of the investigation. The skull's nose had been chewed by a bear, but was otherwise whole. The crash had taken place in the hunting unit for her tag and the bull was legal, so she was allowed to keep it. It was back to Bismarck by the end of January. The skull's presence in her room reminded her of the courage and grit that emerged from the young woman in the Alaskan bush. She thought of Theodore Roosevelt's quote after an assasination attempt, "...it takes more than that to kill a bull moose."

She applied for and was drawn for a turkey tag in North Dakota, which gave her two things. First, it was a goal to work towards. She needed to design a system that would accommodate her disability. Second, it was a chance to get back outdoors after a long winter. Her dad helped her with a system to hunt with one arm for the spring turkey season. It was difficult, but she was ready for opening day the second Saturday in April. Her gobbler was tagged that afternoon. She was stronger and more confident than ever.

Elizabeth was fitted for a prosthetic in May and could barely contain her excitement. The list of demands was long for the company that designed it. First, it needed to allow her to shoot. Second, she needed to be able to cast a line. It was important to her to continue to be out in nature and harvesting her own food. Her whole life was ahead of her, and she would not let this disability define her. She would not play the victim; she was the hero.

ACKNOWLEDGEMENT

I would like to thank those who have taken me hunting my whole life. A special thanks to my dad, who we lost too early. Also the Anderson family for including me in their hunts after Dad died. The antler in the cover was provided by Dayle A; thanks! I am grateful to my wife who helped edit and improve this manuscript. Any mistakes are my own. A special thanks to Jim Thoreson for teaching me all I know about meat processing. Finally, an enormous thank you to all of my teachers over the past 33 years. There are too many to mention. You have all opened the world to a small-town kid from North Dakota.

ABOUT THE AUTHOR

Eric Viall

Eric Viall is a science educator in rural North Dakota. He has spent his life hunting, fishing, reading, and studying science. He has two little girls, a dog, and an incredibly patient wife. He enjoys typewriters and cooking.